The Legend of the Gamesmen

The Dim Continent

Book 3 of The Legend of the Gamesmen

Jo Sparkes

PORTLAND, OREGON

The Dim Continent - Jo Sparkes – 1rst Ed.
ISBN 978-0-9853318-8-7

For my Dad.

Special thanks to Annie Tapper Blem — artist extradordinaire - for her fabulous covers.

And to Mike Terlizzi, for his wonderful maps.

Prologue

IT WAS PITCH BLACK. Scraping his hand against a rough post, Lump clamped his jaw tight to keep from cursing.

Any normal harbor had torches burning through the night. Providing light so sailors could find their ships on the dock, and vessels at sea knew land was nearby. But this harbor master was either ignorant or catered to those preferring to remain unseen.

Lump had known the type of work he took on when Kratchett first paid him - known and been satisfied. This sort of employment did not please all, which meant it paid more. More still if one was smart and kept his tongue between his teeth. And Lump was very smart.

At least, he'd thought so before finding himself

skulking around a dark harbor on a foggy night.

Feeling his way past a pile of stacked crates, he trod out onto the wharf just as a lantern appeared on the hill.

He slipped back behind the crates.

The lantern swung gently as the bearer made his way down the street. Whoever it was moved silently - and even as the light drew close, the flame revealed no more than booted feet beneath rippling cloaks. Hard to guess it was two people.

Still, Lump knew it was Kratchett and Rain.

He'd been sent for, commanded to meet them here. No further information had been conveyed, but then he guessed they were in a rush.

He held his tongue as the pair drew even with his hiding place.

"Where is that fool?" Rain hissed. Lump had little doubt she was referring to him.

"Probably on board," Kratchett said, in that calm voice he used when handling her. "We can trust Lump." And Kratchett guided her up the gangplank.

Lump shifted, ready to follow, when a faint drumming grew in the distance. Horses, he realized. But they sounded slightly wrong.

The moon drifted out above the fog as hooves pounded down the cobbled street. Lump spied Kratchett and Rain at the ship's rail before he turned to see riders leaping off mounts, racing towards them. Abandoning their steeds - including one giant beast that dwarfed the rest. The exhausted horses stood untethered and uncertain.

Men - he didn't try to count, but more than ten - swarmed onto the ship. Leaving behind one large thing.

One very large Thing.

Lump had a flashing impression of hair and fangs before the moon slipped mercifully back into cloud cover. He would never be sure he hadn't dreamt the whole event.

But dream or no, he let the vessel sail away without him.

1.

TRYST STOOD at the arch opening, gazing out from the council chamber to the mountain that guarded the rear of the Palace. Growing up he'd imagined the ragged cliff as a giant Defense Master, protecting his home. Strong and invincible - like his father, the King.

Now his own Defense Master chased information, preparing to follow the creature that had masqueraded as King Bactor. A creature from the Dim Continent, with evil intent and motives unknown. Jason sought to uncover those motives. The trail, so he said, would be easier to follow if they knew the thing's goals.

Footsteps behind him forced him back to the present. "Majesty. King Ganny arrives in the courtyard."

Tryst turned and nodded.

In his time away from the Palace titles had become foreign things - and now he found their conventions annoying. With his father gone, he was suddenly 'liege' or 'majesty'. Being so addressed only served to remind him the man was missing and in danger.

But surely not dead. The enemy hadn't killed Tryst when it had the chance. King Bactor *must* be alive.

Pushing away from the arch, he strode toward the stairs. There was still time before King Ganny would alight from his massive coach, but Tryst yearned to see him.

King Ganny was no longer King at all. He was Tryst's grandsire.

Striding too fast for the guard at the courtyard door, Tryst had to force himself to wait without glaring at the tardy sentry. Such delays had never annoyed him before his time on the Wavering Continent.

Or perhaps he'd never been in that great a hurry.

The heavy oak portal swung wide to reveal sunshine and four coaches crowding the welcoming area. Sixteen steaming horses pawed the cobblestone while postilions yelled for assistance and servants hauled away wardrobe trunks, hat boxes, and anything else the elder King might demand to aid his comfort. Indeed, three grunting attendants wrested a throne-like chair from atop a carriage.

Tryst stepped down the entrance steps as a fifth coach rolled in, the coat of arms blazing on its massive

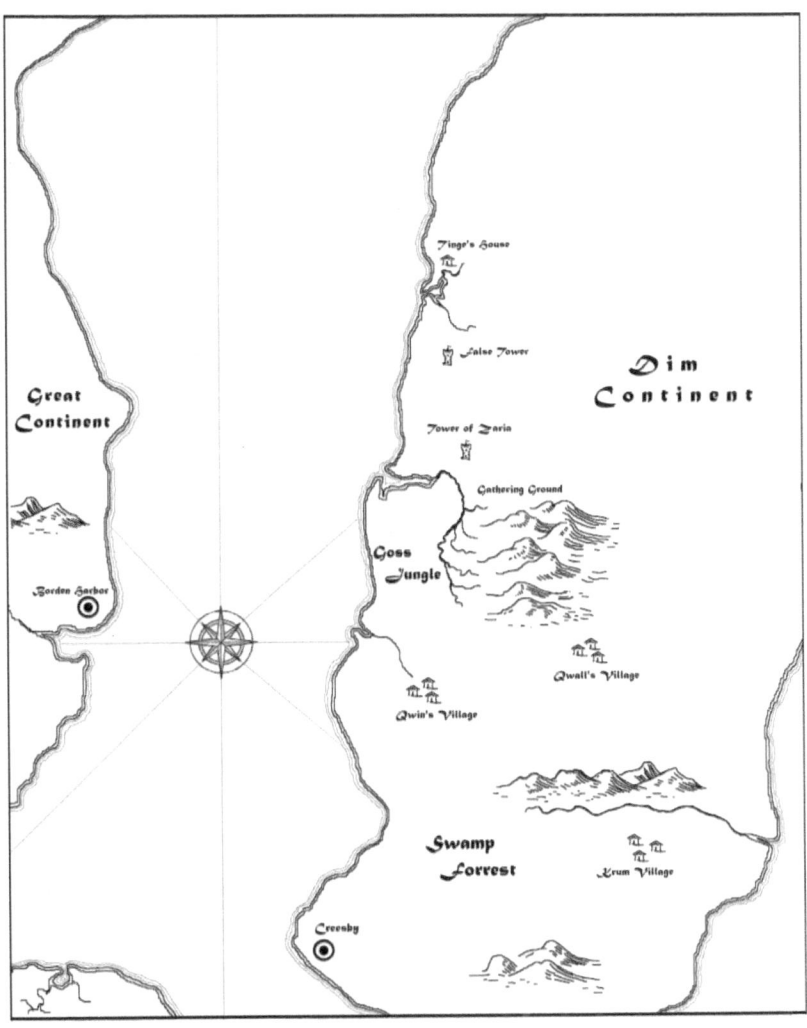

doors. No less than eight perfectly matched black steeds stamped in harness now, nostrils flaring not at the work but at the forced stop. His grandsire's animals could race for many miles.

A liveried servant leapt off the high-perched seat, bowed to Tryst, and yanked open the coach door with a peculiar flourish.

Silence.

And then from within a stirring, and King Ganny alighted.

Tryst was small for a Skullan; his father was considered above average. But King Ganny - in all his life Tryst never heard the name Ganny without the 'King' title before it - stood half a head taller than any Skullan Tryst had ever seen. He was a massive mountain of a man that age had yet to diminish.

Standing beside the elder king made Tryst feel like a perennial ten-year-old.

"Well, young Tryst, I see you've not yet grown to manhood."

"I fear, Grandsire, I am now as much as I shall ever be."

"Doubtful," snorted the King, allowing Tryst to grasp his arm in a custom favored by those of his generation. "Now tell me what you've done with your father."

"ATHAN! ATHAN! ATHAN!"
Marra looked around the Black Arena, seeing the

thousands of spectators on their feet, screaming the name of the Black Tide's leader.

"He relies too much on defending the comet tail," Drail murmured, his eyes riveted - as were those of Wolfbur and Old Merle - on the playing field below.

"The man's defense is most impressive," Old Merle nodded. "But you'd do better to use your own strengths. With your accuracy, take your shots at the cone."

"You'd do better to concentrate on defeating Trumen teams," Wolfbur's guttural voice cut through the cheers, "than strategizing for an opponent you will never face."

Marra sighed, and forced herself to watch.

The Gold Harbor Arena - the greatest comet arena in all of Missea - was hosting a week of Coronation Games, and this was only day three. She'd quickly discovered that observing continual competitions of Skullan teams held far less excitement than watching Drail and the Hand of Victory play.

In truth, she'd rather be playing with her potions at the Agben School. She'd told that to Kirth, her Skullan mentor, and found herself thrust from the workroom out into the sunshine. Kirth said it was because Marra worked too long over her herbs, like a dog worrying a bone, and needed a break.

Marra thought it was because Kirth grew tired of her questions.

Marra had spent more than a year helping Drail to

follow in his grandsire's footsteps. He yearned to be the best gamesman of his generation, and prove it by defeating Skullan in the Gold Harbor Arena. Also called the Black Arena because of the odd look the pouring of obsidian stone had given it, this was the site where his grandsire had battled Skullan in a game legendary to both races. Drail was the first Trumen to defeat a Skullan team, as far as anyone knew, but he'd since discovered that those Skullan roaming the desert were not near the level of skill as the gamesmen here in Missea.

Marra's Birr Elixir helped him, or so he told her. He'd named her Brista, potions maker to the Hand of Victory, after she'd brewed the recipe from her dead mistress's book. In return Drail had rescued her from a lonely desert town and a bad man, bringing her here to the one place she could continue learning.

She desperately wanted to repay him, and hoped to discover mixtures more useful than a simple energy brew. But she couldn't do that sitting here watching these endless comet games. She needed to keep studying at the Agben School.

"CEASE!" cried the Judge.

Marra realized she'd missed the winning shot. No need to wonder who had won - Athan's stance on the field declared his victory as no handful of words could.

"I want to play him," Drail insisted. "Wolfbur, how did you obtain status enough to play in the Black Arena?"

"Three years of victories were not enough," the weathered Skullan told him. "So my team left Missea to roam the Great Continent. To play every town, every village. A year later, we returned with triumphs both real and exaggerated, and mounted a worthy challenge."

Marra saw the soft smile on Drail's lips. "We've acted the role of traveling gamesmen before."

"Trumen on a Trumen land," Old Merle eyed him skeptically. "How many Trumen games even exist beyond the city gates? And why should winning those impress any Skullan?"

Trumen, the smaller of the two races, were considered inferior in every way to the ruling Skullan people. Skullan stood a third larger, taller and more massive. Their king ruled the land - although the Wavering Continent, the desert home to Marra and Drail, saw little of actual Skullan reign.

"I'd like to see what lies beyond the city," Manten grinned.

Marra thought of her study at Agben, and sighed.

When the games had finished, Marra slipped away.

The cobblestones were slick from the recent rain, but her new slippers bore the Missean sole and gripped the stone well. She hurried down the ramp to the Palace side entrance, dug out her key, and entered.

Tryst, the Skullan Prince, had given her this key. She hadn't used it since the moon had waned, and even now hesitated to do so. There were vials in her Palace chamber however, and as glass was dear and she'd broken a flask yesterday, the least she could do was replace it.

As she passed through a Royal garden, Marra noticed the banyon tree under whose leaves she and Tryst used to sit. No one sat there now, so she sped on to her room.

Tryst had been a friend and companion, even a gamesman with Drail's Hand of Victory. At the time none of them had known he was Skullan, let alone a prince, until he fought to claim his rightful place in the Palace. He'd gained his throne and lost his father.

Now he worked tirelessly to find King Bactor. He no longer needed their aid, and hadn't sought them out.

Marra grasped the handle, clicked the latch, and stood on the threshold of her own private room.

It was a coveted courtyard chamber, highly sought in the Palace. The King himself had honored her with it - or perhaps it was the Terrin who had taken his place that had done so. The Terrin - a creature from the Dim Continent - was discovered just a moon ago to be posing as the King. The impostor had escaped.

Now the sun pouring through the open balcony doors danced on the glass vials, sparkling merrily. Even though she hadn't been here in a moon, those outside doors were always flung open on sunny days and shut against the rain and the night by the servants who swept the dust from the place. In all honesty, she couldn't fathom the extravagance of Palace ways. What was the point of cleaning a room every day when no one used it for months?

The tap of her heels against the stone floor muted as she strode across the thick blue carpet. Voices drifted in from the garden as she plucked the vials from the polished wood.

"Young Jason leads the search for your father? Why not Klangor? He's never failed."

"Klangor retired years ago." Tryst's reply held a peculiar deference, laced with a weariness Marra had never heard before. She bit her lip, realizing how Tryst must feel. Alone.

He'd finally come home after more than a year - to find himself alone yet again. It was a feeling she knew herself. Impulsively she walked out to the balcony.

"But young Jason..."

"Is the Defense Master of the realm. There is no one I trust...no one more trustworthy, Grandsire."

Already cross the terrace, Marra halted at that last word. But her intrusion was noted by both men poised below her. Tryst - with his head shaved in the Skullan fashion - actually smiled at her. The other man did not.

The height of the balcony did not diminish the man's stature, for he towered over Tryst. What stopped her cold was not his size but his demeanor - for few Skullan would glare at her after their own prince's welcome.

And glare this man did. "You may go back to your cleaning, girl," he said, and even standing below her still looked down his nose.

"Grandsire, this is Marra," Tryst touched his grandfather's arm. "The Brista who saved my life. Marra, may I present His Majesty, King Ganny. Skullan ruler for forty years. The father of my father."

Marra sank into a curtsy, attempting to imitate the court ladies she had witnessed. From King Ganny's look, she knew she had failed.

"You have our gratitude for your service to Missea," the elder's voice did not thaw one wit. "Now leave us."

"Stay." Tryst stepped forward, startling both her and his grandsire. "I've wanted to talk to you. Is there a way for you to sweep the Palace for any other Terrin influence?"

Staring at Tryst, she caught the same stare on King Ganny's face, and almost laughed aloud.

"Please?"

Something in his tone released her smile. "I'll do my best, Tryst."

"Majesty," King Ganny barked. "He is Majesty to you."

Marra nodded, and fled.

Tryst watched her slip through the balcony doors. He knew that nervous withdrawal, that need of hers not to disturb anyone or anything around her.

"Trumen have grown too puffed up in themselves," his grandsire growled.

"That Trumen risked her life to help a stranger in the desert. It was a year before she knew I was Skullan, let alone Prince."

King Granny snorted in disbelief, and Tryst felt his fingers clench into fists. "Females," the old king told him, "have a certain sense for self-preservation."

Picturing his ragged appearance on the Flats of Beard, slumped by a campfire beside the victorious Drail and his gamesmen, Tryst suddenly relaxed and grinned.

"If she could sense that, then she's the one we want scouring the place for Terrin traces."

Clapping his grandsire's shoulder, Tryst marched him past an interested guard.

Spying the walls of Agben in the distance, Marra sped along the third tier walkway.

Missea had almost as many avenues above the ground as on it, and while she still found it dizzying to travel high above the streets, the quickest route often stood several stories in the air. Landmarks were easier to see, distances better judged. And as the horses drawing supplies or more affluent passengers trotted only on the ground level, walkways avoided both them and their droppings.

She darted down the ramp to the shadowed doorway hidden behind a trellis of almost black vines.

A 'Wiskett Bramble', she'd learned in class. Useless plant, so Leah said, yet it smelled potent to Marra.

The door led to a sheltered corner in the vast garden of Agben. The School of Agben studied the art of herbs, of crafting potions, balms, and elixirs. Marra had not yet completed her first year - but she'd learned more than properties of plants. She'd learned that she loved it.

She loved to create an elixir that helped strengthen a comet team, or a salve to ease muscle strain. To scour the outdoors for the right plants, to select the best leaves. To do something Drail and the others couldn't do for themselves.

To be useful.

The sun already brushed the west wall, and she smelled dinner cooking in the south kitchen. Classes would be done for the day, so she headed for the subterranean cave no student should know existed.

Kirth, an elder teacher of Agben, knelt beside a white snowdrop flower in the coldest of the cave-rooms. The Skullan woman had her back to the doorway, but Marra was not surprised when she spoke.

"Footsteps too eager to be anyone but Marra." The elder's breath formed a white cloud, so cold was the room. "Now what can that girl want today?"

Circling around her teacher, Marra peered down into the pale blue eyes. "Tryst - the Prince - asked me if I could sweep the Palace for...Terrin traces."

"Indeed?" Kirth pushed herself up, taking a moment to straighten one knee. "Did he seek this help from Agben? Or from a mere student?"

"He saw me at the Palace. The thought only just occurred." Marra bit her lip. "Can Agben help?"

Kirth raised an eyebrow. "If any are ill, we can seek to cure. Agben studies the discipline to heal, and the discipline to enhance."

The familiar words hung in the air. Taking a deep breath, Marra asked the question that had teased her for several moons. "Is there a third discipline?"

Kirth's eyes narrowed, but her lips only thinned.

Marra knew she tread unwelcome ground, but having started decided to continue. "Rain did so much more than that. Her mixture changed color when a particular person drew near. And something made us believe a Terrin creature was King Bactor." Rain, a powerful Woman of Agben, had committed treason against her own race, the Skullan people.

"She garnered no such knowledge within these walls." Kirth's eyes were hard. "Brews of that sort are unnatural. The essence of evil. They're forbidden."

"But - why?"

Kirth latched onto Marra's arm and marched her out of the cavern.

She stopped when they reached the first cave with the fire pit and the worktable. And sat herself down on the lone stool.

"Marra, there is a harmony to life that we must

honor. A proper, natural balance. The essence of Agben is discovering how to restore the body to its perfect balance. Rain's witch-work seeks to rip that apart."

"But we cannot counter such powerful creations with healing balms!"

"Did you not use healing mixtures to cure the Prince of a most powerful evil?"

Marra shook her head. "I was just lucky."

"My child, any discipline, any endeavor can be pursued with the intent to do good, or otherwise. Pursuing good causes with bad actions is no different than pursuing bad causes. You cannot achieve good through bad actions. You've already tainted the very goal you seek."

Arguments sprang to Marra's tongue, but she did not speak. She knew from past experience that Kirth would not be moved.

And there was another topic hovering on the elder Skullan's lips, one that had been there for some days. Even now her teacher hesitated.

And then the question came. "Marra, what do you remember of Britta's last days?"

It was early afternoon when the heavens seemed to burst open. Sheets of rain hurtled from the sky, shrouding the city in a dense wet veil.

Lump strode the cobblestones quickly, welcoming the downpour and the wind. Less Misseans trod the streets in such weather, which meant less eyes observed him pass. He didn't know how much the Elite Guard had guessed - Kratchett had continually underestimated their abilities.

He couldn't now afford the same mistake.

South of the Warehouse District and farther from the Old Gate, the oldest area of Missea seemed to crowd in upon itself, as if the newer parts had shoved these buildings too close together. Here there were only three tiers, and the bridges swayed on ropes instead of the solid wide paths constructed through the rest of the city.

It was home to the dock workers, day laborers and the like. What Kratchett often termed the common man. The streets had been cobblestone once, but not so firmly made. Now gaping holes peppered the road, and the sodden dirt produced deep mud pools for the unwary.

Shops were few and far between. Most did not bother with signs to declare their existence - some from lack of need to advertise, and some from lack of will. The second story door, accessible only from a teetering stack of old crates, fell into the latter category.

Lump scanned the area carefully before ascending the makeshift stairway and slipping inside.

Fenna's front room consisted of a pallet, a three-legged stool, and shelves of pottery jars. It was supposed to be a healing place, but as no broom nor dust cloth had touched it in many a day, the atmosphere was more desolation than hope.

There was no sign of Fenna.

Lump reached into his hidden coat pocket to grasp the dagger handle, and then crept towards the first opening. Fenna's place, as others in this district, was laid out in tiny rooms linked like beads on a bracelet - door after door leading to room after room, until you wound up back at the beginning.

Weapon ready, he slipped the latch - which was ominous in its silence - and passed into the next room. Her main store of herbs filled this chamber.

On his guard now, Lump paused to check the larger containers, scanning any place just deep enough to hide a small woman. He always thought Fenna to be merely Rain's pigeon, but in his experience, well-oiled doors in otherwise unkempt places hinted at dark deeds.

A long crate lay in a far corner. He stepped carefully to it, making sure it was too close to the wall to hide anyone behind. And then on impulse, he removed the sacks covering it and lifted the lid.

What he saw chilled him to his core.

"Climbing crates to enter a shop? She must not get many visitors," Marra frowned. The stack seemed unstable, and she feared for Kirth's safety.

Kirth, however, never hesitated. When the elder reached the top and opened the door, Marra reluctantly followed.

The interior looked no more inviting. It wasn't the dirt so much as the smell. And the faint noises - somehow ominous.

"Mistress..." Marra began, but Kirth waved an impatient hand and stepped on to the next room.

Marra stayed where she was, puzzled by the smell. It was familiar and not unpleasant, which was odd for such a dingy place. It reminded her of...Tryst.

A second door opened - one she hadn't noticed. For an instant she thought Kirth was returning, until she saw the boots. Boots she recognized, boots that had dogged her path. No fox was etched on the inside leather - but these had oft accompanied that other pair.

Lump, she remembered. His name was Lump - Kratchett's man to do his dirty work.

Lump was shoving something in his shirt pocket, and from both the way he handled it and the tanged aroma in the air, she knew it wasn't good.

And then he noticed her. His eyes widened, and then narrowed as he took a silent step towards her.

"Marra," Kirth called. Her voice sounded distant - too far to help her. But it was enough.

Lump fled.

She ought to have run to the door, to at least see which way he ran, but Marra didn't move. She vaguely registered the sounds of those boots speeding off through the rain.

"Marra!"

Shaking herself, she hurried to Kirth.

The second room was storage, although not like the storage rooms of Agben, or even Britta's shop on the desert Flats. Here crates and jars littered the floor, seemingly left in the first spot available. It lacked the organization of Agben storerooms, and Marra wondered how anyone could locate anything they needed.

The first true signs of habitation appeared in the third room.

A mattress lay in the corner, and though it lacked a bed frame it was covered with a faded blue and white quilt someone had spent time stitching. A table held both an oil lamp and a teapot, with a worn kettle sitting upon a tiny stove nearby. A shelf held several jars, including one with a bunch of wildflowers thrust inside. To sweeten the air, she realized.

The sweetness had long since died.

The lamp was lit - which was a good thing as no windows broke the dingy expanse of wall. Kirth knelt near the stove, and as Marra approached, she saw that the flash of green on the floor was not a rug but a skirt.

"Fetch me a clean cloth, if such a thing exists in the place."

The green skirt belonged to a tiny woman, face pinched, eyes closed. The tiny woman's blouse was not of scarlet material as first appeared, for the color darkened before her eyes.

Blood.

Whirling, Marra sped to the clothes pegs near the mattress, which held a surprising selection of blouses, all fine linen and clean. Marra snatched a white one and knelt by Kirth.

"Not...that one," the tiny woman murmured. Kirth used it anyway, pressing against the woman's chest.

It rapidly turned red.

"See if you can find camphor juice," Kirth hissed.

"Too late," the injured woman sighed. She turned her eyes to Marra. "I was just to watch him," she whispered. "Just to watch and apply more balm to the nostrils if he stirred."

Marra's stomach iced over. The aroma, the familiar smell.

"Never told me...but I guessed who he was. The Prince..." The last word escaped her body in a long sigh, and no more air was drawn in to replace it.

"Never mind the camphor juice." Kirth leaned back on her heels.

Marra leapt up, as much to retreat from the dead woman as anything. Kirth rose more slowly. "Fenna, an old student," she sighed. "Years back she assisted Britta on certain...things. I rather hoped to find an answer or two." Kirth checked the kettle, and leaning over a single basin, poured the water over one hand and then the other.

Marra drifted back to the storage room.

Drying her fingers on an old dishrag, Kirth

followed. "Why do you suppose she spoke of the Prince?"

Scanning the area, Marra threaded her way round crates and large pottery jars. "Perhaps she'd heard rumors of his disappearance."

"But the Prince is safe in the Palace."

Marra struggled to lift the top off a long box where the odor was strongest. After a moment, Kirth joined her. Together they raised the lid.

"Great Goose guide me," Kirth breathed.

King Bactor lay inside. For a long moment he seemed dead, until she caught the shallow rise of his chest.

"When we first found Tryst...in that unnatural sleep..." Marra turned to stare at Kirth. "This is that same smell."

Kirth leaned close, resting a palm on his chest, prying open his eyelid. "And you woke a man in this state?"

Marra nodded.

Kirth looked at her in wonder. "You might need to do it again."

They dined in the council chamber.

King Ganny insisted, siting the lovely view. Tryst was not surprised, however, when his grandsire offered a different reason once they were seated and alone.

"Here we can be sure of no accidental

eavesdropping." He dipped a soda biscuit into his creamed gravy. "So there is no knowing how long your father has been gone?"

Tryst toyed with his swoopfish in spice sauce - but found no appetite. "I believe he was taken sometime after I became Prince again. Otherwise the need to hunt me down would not have been so severe."

"So, likely he's been gone more than a moon," King Ganny frowned. "And with no expectation of discovery."

"The Defense Master pursues leads in the Nirr Provence, and then sets sail."

King Ganny shook his head. "Send a ship now, with someone to investigate. Your Defense Master can follow."

"But we don't even know which port to land...the Dim Continent is vast."

His grandsire eyed him in small amusement. "It is, young Tryst. But only the port of Creesby allows non-terrin."

A servant tapped before entering, to check the state of their meal. Tryst beckoned for more wine; King Ganny shooed him away. The old man's eyes never left Tryst - but he didn't speak again until the door swung shut.

"I myself negotiated the trade agreement when I was your age. Anything we send them - every ship, in fact, must arrive at that single port. You'll find Skullan and Trumen live there, work there. Beyond that port neither race is welcome."

Tryst could only gape.

King Ganny smiled gently. "You thought, perhaps, the entire Dim Continent was part of the Skullan Empire. On parchment, Creesby is Skullan. Fifty years ago few of its citizens acknowledged that - and I doubt the sentiments have changed."

The door burst open and Jason came striding into the room. Furious, King Ganny whirled to see who dared approach. Tryst prepared to defend his friend - and then saw the flash in the man's eyes.

"Your pardon, majesties. King Bactor is found and being brought to the Palace."

Tryst was on his feet without knowing how he got there.

"Alive?" King Ganny barked hoarsely.

"Asleep."

It seemed Marra spent forever alone in that dismal dwelling with a dead woman and a sleeping King. Kirth had wanted to send her for help - but they both doubted she could find Fenna's place again.

Leah returned with the elder just a blink of the sun before the Elite Guard poured in. A heated argument sprang up around the most dignified way to carry their King, before the Guard Captain lifted the sleeping monarch in his arms. A cape was wrapped around the man - so his subjects would not see his vulnerability - and in a flash the room was empty.

Fenna's removal was less conspicuous.

Marra had thought that was the end of it. To her surprise, however, she was summoned to the Palace three days later.

"Prepare your cure," Kirth said, and Marra did. Earlier she'd been told the Agben healers would take care of the King.

"Apparently," Kirth sighed, "they cannot naturally heal that which was unnaturally done."

So Marra prepared the inhalant, adding the Trevor seed, and plied it carefully. There was no effect.

The next day she tried the mint brew she had first used. It was a liquid, thus difficult to administer. And no effect. That afternoon she made the inhalant without her added ingredients, and still Tryst's father slept.

On the third day she tried the Trevor seed inhalant again. King Bactor stirred, but never woke. Marra repeated the inhalant two more days, under Kirth's caution to limit the dosage to once a day.

He was waking, she could tell, but slower than Tryst had done. "Because he is older?" she asked Kirth.

The elder rolled her eyes. "This was administered much more recently. Perhaps more thoroughly, given your success with the Prince."

While Marra administered to the King she stayed in the Palace. Tryst visited frequently, always accompanied by King Ganny.

And King Ganny did not like her.

"Are you stretching this out, girl?" he demanded at one point. "Wake him now!"

Tryst set a hand on the old king's shoulder. "Peace, grandsire. She is Agben, and doing what is right for her King."

Marra pressed her lips together. Tryst was wrong on two counts: she was not Agben, but a student. And no matter what anyone claimed, she couldn't think of Bactor as her King. He was Skullan, and she'd never known of his existence before she arrived in Missea.

"Kirth believes it best to wake him slowly, Majesty."

After the two men left she straightened, rubbing the small of her back where an ache had suddenly arisen.

King Ganny seemed to hate her, and she found that most unsettling. Tryst - Skullan though he was - had never treated her as anything less than an equal. Even King Bactor had been kind, although come to think of it, she couldn't be sure she'd ever met King Bactor. It was possible all the courtesy had come from the Terrin impostor.

Later, when Marra slipped outside to walk in the garden, a young Skullan girl approached. Others did take in the beauty of the Palace grounds, but none had ever approached her before.

"You are the healer to the King?" she asked, her eyes alight with something. The girl seemed younger than Marra, though of course she towered over her. Her long black hair cascaded down her back in Skullan fashion, and her dress was a vivid blue.

Marra found herself envying both her dress and her poise. "Yes, lady," she nodded.

"Wake him soon," the girl grinned. "So that heavenly prince will notice my new wardrobe."

Marra realized her mouth was gaping - and snapped it shut.

"He's too wrapped up in that," the girl explained, as if talking to a friend. "Even at dinner he's distracted. My name is Karna."

"Marra," she replied, once she realized Karna was waiting for her to speak. No Skullan outside of Agben had ever asked her anything. Except Tryst.

"Prince Tryst is gorgeous," Karna giggled, "even if he is short. Though I guess he's not short to you. Do you like Skullan men?"

"Marra," Kirth called from the balcony.

"I...I have to go," Marra apologized.

The girl nodded, her eyes friendly. "Maybe I'll see you later."

A young Skullan lady, treating her as an equal while confessing her admiration for the Prince. Seemingly both warm and kind.

For some reason Marra disliked her.

Catching this Lump fellow was not difficult. Jason faced the man in a Palace dungeon within three days.

The dark cell had its usual effect. The man's shoulders were slumped, eyes watering at the unaccustomed torchlight. Still, he wasn't broken.

Jason's next step usually employed an Agben Woman or Zaria priest. He reluctantly discarded them, though he hated to do so. Both had a way of intimidating prisoners, and Zaria swore it had Truth Diviners able to detect lies.

But Zaria often had an agenda of its own, rarely providing everything promised. He'd been relying on the Tower less and less.

And Agben appeared just a little too often in this trail of conspiracy. Tryst had a fondness for Marra and trusted her - but she was a mere apprentice and not privy to the plots of the elders.

As it turned out, however, the prisoner was more than ready to talk.

"My orders were to pick up a sleeping man in an herb shop on the Flats of Beard," he said without prodding. "Didn't know who he was - didn't care to ask."

"So you committed high treason without knowing why."

"Never touched him at all. He was gone afore we took him."

"Why the desert? Such a long way to send the Prince. And where were you taking him?"

Lump leaned back against his cell wall, too relaxed for Jason's taste. "Orders were to board a vessel in Port Leet. When we failed to secure him, that Agben wench canceled the passage - leaving us high and dry. Wound up sleeping in a cargo hold on a small schooner."

"Agben?" Jason kept the word casual.

"Catrona, she called herself. Waiting for us in Port Leet. She threatened the little Brista, but not well enough."

That Lump's words cleared Marra made it easier for Jason to believe him. The little herb girl was guileless and had had many chances to betray Tryst if that had been her goal.

But yet another Agben name. They would have to tread carefully with the Women.

"Was this ship sailing for Missea? Or for the Dim Continent?"

For the first time emotion flashed across Lump's face.

"I was never told. Expected a lesser port on the Great Continent. If I'd known 'bout that hairy beast..."

Jason stepped close, studying the man's face. When Lump looked up, traces of horror roiled in his eyes.

"Suppose to sail with them a fortnight back. From Borden Harbor in the Nirr Provence. First time I ever saw one of those.

"Big it was, a true monster. Long, spindly legs. Figured I'd likely be caught staying behind - but better that than trapped in a ship with that thing."

That last was a lie - the man had thought to avoid capture. But what he told of the Terrin was real, or Lump thought was real.

"Who went on the Terrin vessel?"

"Kratchett and the Agben Rain. Along with ten or

so palace guard."

"And King Bactor?"

"Didn't have nothing to do with him."

"But you were there, where he was found."

"I was there to...for another purpose. Never knew anything about the King."

Jason suspected the man wasn't entirely truthful - and most of his information merely confirmed what they already believed. It would be well to see Lump thoroughly questioned.

But liar or no, a fourth Agben name had been added to the list of traitors.

She hurried to the sleeping king - but he hadn't changed. His breathing was the same, his position unaltered.

"King Bactor will be fine," Kirth said. "But I have spoken to King Ganny."

Marra sighed. She was beginning to dislike King Ganny.

"He seems to believe Agben itself 'tis involved in this plot."

"Rain was involved. Agben was not."

Kirth paced the room, her skirt rippling purposefully along the plush red carpet. Revealing a disquiet that startled Marra. Surely no one could think Agben had anything to do with this Terrin intrigue?

"Fenna was also involved," Kirth said slowly. "And now the King informs me not only was Catrona helping them in Port Leet...the kidnapped Prince was on his way to Britta."

Marra nodded. "I thought you knew, Mistress. Tryst was found in the back of the shop. But Britta had been dead for five weeks - surely it was Snark, her brother, who did this thing."

Kirth's frown did not diminish. "Perhaps. But no less than four Agben women come in to this tale. And then, in the Palace eyes at least, there's you."

A cold fear gripped Marra's throat.

Kirth assembled the three most senior women in the east tower table room.

Agben had four towers, one on each corner of the building. Two of those held large rooms at the top level; the other two were divided into smaller sleeping chambers for the most senior women. She herself had such a room.

To Confer was to bring together those whose opinions stood most valued, and present any question with far-reaching consequences. All sides must be thoroughly discussed and explored.

There was space at the round table for twenty-seven women, but it was rare that more than twelve sat. Rain would normally have been invited to Confer, and Kirth winced at the thought. In truth, no one had assembled a Confer for several cycles of seasons. This had seemed to signal how well things stood. Now, however, she wondered if it was due at least partly to the fact that Rain had assumed a leader role.

Agben had no formal leaders or formal roles. Over the years a sort of natural hierarchy developed, where the most senior - and hopefully most wise - among them rose in recognition and respect. The Women sought council from these individuals, and when any concern merited it, a Confer was called. The wisest among them, and those deemed valuable to the dilemma, were then assembled.

The flaw in the system was that Rain had grabbed more and more authority. If someone went to her she handled things herself. Her forcefulness - and indeed her known temper - meant many had naturally gone to her first to avoid problems.

So Kirth summoned Lyra, Magda, and finally old Helen. Helen had long left the School, preferring to spend her waning years with her daughters. Or so she said. Helen lived outside Missean walls, but not so far that she couldn't be summoned within a day.

Lastly, Kirth considered Marra, and might have made her sit outside the room, waiting to be summoned. But she was still bothered by Rain's betrayal of trust, and these flaws in Agben's lack of power structure made her hesitant. Let no one grasp any notions of Marra's place beyond that of a mere student.

When the four assembled at the giant table, necessity to hear forced them to sit close. Perhaps we need another table, Kirth mulled.

"Why are we here?" Lyra whined. Lyra preferred her beakers to people, and her notes to anything else.

"She's annoyed about Rain," Magda screwed up her nose. "I warned her; she listened not. Now she wants to yell at me in front of everyone."

"Rain is gone," Kirth told them. "We can do nothing about her now. But her detritus must be swept clean."

Helen moved slowly, more so than Kirth remembered. Yet her words were sharp and cut through the confusion. "I know nothing of Rain," Helen plunked down heavily in her chair. "Tell me."

So Kirth did. She told her about the kidnapping of King Bactor's heir, and his being taken to the Flats of Beard where Britta kept shop. Rain's stealing of Marra from the school was described, as well as her apparent use of the pink gruel in bowls to identify the Prince once he'd escaped.

"That's nasty Terrin perversion," Helen said.

"You heard of the King himself disappearing? A Terrin somehow made itself seem Skullan, pretending to be His Majesty. And now we've found the true King sleeping in that same unnatural way. At Fenna's place...and she was murdered!"

"We must ban Rain. Send out instructions! She is to be shunned, as Zaria priests shun one of their own!" Lyra cried.

"Turn her over to the Palace guard," Magda insisted. "Rain must be..."

"How many others are involved?" Helen cut through

the argument.

"That's all I know," Kirth said, very glad she'd sent for Helen. "Even Britta's intentions are unknown. She may have helped, but she may have refused. Perhaps even tried to warn us."

"We'll need to talk to all who knew her. Her special students."

"We need you," Kirth told Helen gently. "To find out if we have other problems in Agben."

Helen clamped her lips shut. After a moment, she nodded. "It seems we must also prove ourselves to the Palace again."

"How many know?" Magda hissed.

Kirth suppressed a smile. While Magda savored another's scandal, she abhorred the thought of anyone outside the gates hearing of Agben imperfections. "Few citizens are aware of the facts - but rumors are sometimes worse than truth. Most importantly, the Crown knows."

"We must regain their trust," Lyra said. "A formal envoy, to offer all assistance?"

"We think the same," Kirth smiled. "At this moment we're working hard to wake the King. But that merely rights a wrong they believe we committed."

"We must tell the Crown of Tinge," Helen said.

Kirth gaped, before she caught herself. "Agben swore a vow never to do so."

"We swore never to reveal the location nor the knowledge shared," Helen countered. "But that it exists, what they practice...the King now needs to know this."

"You're splitting hairs," Magda said.

"It's our loyalty that cannot be split." Helen's fragile fist hit the table. They all fell silent, staring at her. "You worry the King will doubt our honor, our loyalty. He fears exactly this sort of thing...hiding information that renders him vulnerable to a powerful foe. Tell me, who goes there now?"

Kirth closed her eyes. "Rain has made the last seven trips."

All the women gasped - though Magda and Lyra already knew. Were, in fact, in on the choice.

"If we are to clean our cupboards, someone must go now."

Kirth sighed. "Perhaps we could send..."

"You," Helen told her. "We send you."

2.

THAT EVENING, TRYST watched as Marra held another inhalant under his father's nose.

Bactor's nostrils twitched, and Tryst held his breath. But the King did not wake.

Sensing his concern, the girl peered up at him. "He is coming round. Another day, maybe two, and your father will truly open his eyes."

Tryst smiled. To everyone else in the Palace, this was their king. Only Marra and his grandsire referred to the man as Tryst's kin.

She shook the vial, holding it in place again. But the King's face made no further reaction.

"Tryst," Jason called from beyond the balcony doors. Tryst strode through them, to find the Defense Master standing on the garden path. "We may have a lead on

Rain. It seems she boarded a ship late at night. In Borden Harbor."

"As we thought. Was the Terrin with her?"

Jason nodded. "So we are told. The informant is but one man with a strong need to preserve his skin. Still, I believe him."

Tryst vaulted the balcony rail, moving away from the King's room. No need to disturb Marra or his father.

"His name," Jason said, "Is Lump."

Marra heard Jason, of course, but couldn't very well rush away. So she shook the vial again, till the odor masked the aroma of the multitude of flowers in the room, and thrust it back beneath the King's nostrils.

The brew had weakened, none-the-less. There was no more reaction.

When the door opened, she didn't bother turning round. She assumed it was Tryst returning.

"I'll have no more of this prissying about, girl. Wake my son and go back to your witch's school."

Marra forced herself to straighten before turning around. In truth the old king scared her, but she'd not back down. This was Tryst's father, after all.

"Majesty, this must be done carefully. It's a very powerful mixture."

He stepped closer, threatening. But she was used to Skullan looming above her, Marra reminded herself. And he could scarcely harm her as she worked on his son.

Instead she turned away to shake the vial one more time and hold it under Bactor's nose.

"You will stay away from Tryst," King Ganny rumbled, his tone quieter yet somehow more threatening.

Startled, Marra stared back.

"He'll dally with Skullan females of a class far beyond your sort. His marriage shall be to royalty. There can be no divergence from that - no stable-born brat to amuse those who seek skeletons in shadows. You cannot tempt him from his proper path."

Slowly his words penetrated. Marra gaped at him, reading the sincerity in his face.

Her hand trembled, and she yanked it away from the King just before the vial shattered.

Blood oozed from her palm. Moving to the table, she found a rag and a basin of water. Somehow the silence came to her aid, giving her a moment to assemble words.

King Ganny, on the other hand, was slightly disconcerted. Whether from her blood or her calm she couldn't guess.

With her hand wrapped, she turned to faced him. "There is no question of such foolishness," she said, her anger escaping despite her best efforts. "I serve Drail, leader of the Hand of Victory. Beside him no Skullan holds any attraction."

Gathering her things, Marra moved to the door. She

clicked the latch, and then looked at the old king from over her shoulder. "He may be Skullan, but he's an honorable man. You do not know Tryst to suggest such nonsense."

She left.

Tryst stood frozen on the balcony.

He wanted to storm in, rip the old man apart. King Ganny might say anything to his grandson - but not to a subject. Not to normal, everyday people who only served their king.

Never to Marra.

What held him back was Jason gripping his arm, forcing him to wait a few blinks of the sun. Allowing them to enter pretending they had heard nothing.

After a few long breaths, Tryst decided his Defense Master was probably right.

It was two days later when King Bactor woke.

His father's movements and memories reminded Tryst of that day in the desert, when he himself had opened his eyes to see a Trumen waif and a band of gamesmen carrying him along like so much extra gear. At that time Tryst had remembered the last hours so vividly he couldn't conceive of having slept at all, let alone the many moons he had been unconscious. Only the distance - finding himself on another continent - had convinced him.

Well, the distance and the fact that his battered

body had completely healed.

Now King Bactor opened his eyes to see Tryst and King Ganny staring down at him as Marra withdrew from the room. "Was I ill?" he smiled.

"Ill?" King Ganny spoke sharply.

"I remember Rain saying something about a fever. Walking down a corridor..."

He frowned, trying to remember.

"How long had I been home, father?" Tryst prodded gently.

"Three days." King Bactor's smile slowly faded. "How long have you been home now?"

Tryst told him.

The next day they assembled in the Council Chamber.

His father chafed at waiting, but Tryst knew the King needed time to clear his head. And it was vital the man be clearheaded for this meeting.

King Ganny was a force unto himself, strong in opinion and rarely recognizing anyone else as worthy of voicing a different view. First Minister Charis, normally a powerful adviser, seemed pliant and ready to bow to the old monarch's dictates.

Jason, the Defense Master, had more understanding than most, but the fact that he had not quite reached his fortieth year was held against him.

Tryst was considered a mere boy.

"We fortify," King Ganny's voice rang out, inviting no opposition.

"Fortification is defense against armies, attacks from without. These attacks came from within." Jason told the room.

"They have been exposed. They must retreat and lick their wounds."

"They did not do so when I escaped in the desert," Tryst replied. "Nor when I took my place in the Palace. Someone went to a lot of trouble to capture one man. Capture him secretly, so no one would notice. And a Terrin was involved."

King Ganny pounded his fist on the table. "The Terrin will pull back from their plans - whatever those were. They will cease now - I know them."

"Give up altogether? Or find another way to achieve their goal?" King Bactor asked. And though his was the quietest voice in the room, authority threaded every word.

King Ganny pursed his lips. "They may be forced to give it up."

"Could a Terrin have just been used?" Tryst looked around the room. "Could the plotters be Skullan? Or even Trumen?"

Charis shook his head. "Terrin do not mix with our races - in truth have never been known to travel off the Dim Continent. Most in Missea consider them a myth. This one did not wander in by mistake."

King Bactor nodded. "There is only one of us who has been to the Dim Continent. Only one who has actually conversed with a Terrin."

Tryst turned to look at his grandsire as King Bactor continued. "Our best course lays not in waiting for their next move - but in making ours. We go to their land to seek out the truth."

King Ganny shook his head. "It's been fifty years since I negotiated the treaty - and it was not a simple thing. Terrin have no king, no capital city. They live in scattered clusters, each with its own ways. Each with its own leader. A ruling council of sorts exists when different leaders meet periodically, at this thing called the Gathering. But it was never effective."

"King Ganny, how would you recommend we proceed?" Jason asked.

Tryst watched the old King's face - the expressions chasing across it. Just when he thought his grandsire would deny answering, the elder sighed. "If you must travel there, travel as gamesmen."

"Gamesmen?!" King Bactor gasped.

"Terrin have an odd culture. They worship luck. They're fascinated with games of chance and sport. Comet gamesmen would draw interest, be tolerated, where others would be shunned."

"Gamesmen," Tryst said. And smiled.

Reading his mind, King Ganny's eyes narrowed. "Mind this - I have known of none to pass the harbor city gate. Terrin distrust Skullan - fear us, despite their huge size. Only Trumen are allowed travel on the Dim Continent."

"Then we should send Trumen..." Tryst began.

"Trumen cannot be trusted with the simplest of tasks," King Ganny glared. "This is the security of the realm."

King Bactor sighed. "My son would not agree. Defense Master, what say you?"

"I would trust Drail - he is an honorable man. The others of his team I cannot vouch for."

"I will vouch for them," Tryst declared.

The discussion boiled over. Taking a cue from his father, Tryst let them argue.

King Ganny abhorred the idea - as he abhorred Trumen. Jason saw possibilities, insisting that to do nothing would lead to future attacks, perhaps more successful ones.

And no one liked the idea of Tryst going.

Which, in the end, decided King Bactor. "There is no one more prepared to seek out this threat, to assess the danger, than the Prince."

"He is the heir to the throne!" King Ganny barked.

"A throne very much in peril."

"At the King's command, I will go." Tryst spoke quietly, yet his firm voice ended the argument. "Allow me then to choose my team."

Twenty blinks of the sun later they rose from the table. Jason himself went to seek the leader of the Hand of Victory.

Drail dropped into a deep stretch. First one hamstring, then easing into the length of the other.

A spicy scent of roses tinged the breeze. It was an open air arena - something he hadn't played in for at least a moon. The more affluent closed arenas drew a better-shod audience, or so they said, but in truth he liked the sky for a roof. Playing in naked sunlight was almost like playing back in the Flats of Beard.

It would be dusk when the game started, when the pink-hued clouds blazed across a crescent moon. Perhaps, Drail mused, his being from the desert meant he watched the sky that Misseans took for granted. Or perhaps with so many sights crowding the Skullan city, its citizens never bothered to look up.

Six levels of stands stood empty with the comet game still an hour away. Only now the second team trod across the field, swapping jokes with the arena owner. Few teams warmed up as the Hand of Victory did.

And few could beat them. None could defeat them consistently.

Drail felt a familiar peace in preparation. All the labor had been done, the practices played, the muscles prepared. There was no more work to do, no more strategy to think upon. All that remained was the game.

He caught a glimpse of red hair darting between posts, a flicker of her skirt behind Manten. Pausing for the blink of the sun, Marra looked over the arena before hurrying to his side.

He smiled. "Does this mean you're done with that

Palace task?"

She nodded.

With the glass sparkling as it caught the sun, he took her offered vial and drank his share of Birr Elixir, before rising from his stretch and handing the potion to Manten. She watched solemnly, so serious as always. Impulsively he reached out to tuck a strand of burnished hair behind her ear.

She gazed up at him, expression unchanging. And he realized he rarely knew what went on in that head of hers.

Manten held the vial aloft and she took it, moving on to administer to the others.

When Fallon had swallowed his portion, he approached Drail. "Manten says you plan to travel soon."

"The sooner the better. Old Merle and Wolfbur plot our route."

Drail intended to travel the Great Continent, playing comet across its length. In doing so he hoped to earn some fame as well as success - a lever to pry his way into games against Skullan teams, as his grandsire had done long ago. It was all he could think of lately.

He was running out of ideas to achieve his Skullan match, and in truth growing tired of Missea. Lately he'd thought of leaving, but returning to the desert held no appeal. To go back felt like a step back. He wanted to go forward.

The young man sighed, squaring his shoulders. "For how long?"

"A full march of seasons. Possibly less."

"I'm not going with you."

Drail slowly digested this. "You have to go."

Fallon shook his head. "Leah and I are to marry. I cannot leave her for a year to wander the continent."

If Fallon bowed out, they'd need to find a replacement. That would take time. And while comet teams on the Great Continent did not value it, Drail had come to realize how crucial it was to have four teammates experienced in playing together. There was a point where a gamesman could anticipate the moves of his friends, know precisely when the ball would come his way, or who best to throw it to.

Fallon's leaving could delay them several moons. It would be after summer, certainly, before they could begin.

"Bring the girl with you."

Fallon looked at him oddly. "She is Agben...at the Agben School."

"So? Marra is as well."

Fallon actually smiled. "And Marra is going with you?"

Drail nodded, surprised at the question.

Fallon stared across the arena, where Marra stood in earnest conversation. "You've asked her? She's willing to give up Agben, to stop her study, just to stand on the sideline while you play?"

"She's not a spectator. Marra is part of the team...has been so since San Cris. She is our Brista."

Fallon's mouth opened again - and then snapped shut as Marra joined them. With a single nod to her, he moved off to stretch.

Marra turned her eyes to Drail. Blue, he realized. A deep blue that could look cold and gray in the wrong light. Now what made him think of that?

"Marra," he said, watching her carefully. "Soon the Hand of Victory leaves the city to wander the Great Continent. To be traveling gamesmen again, as we were in the desert."

Her brows drew down in surprise. Surprise, and something more.

"Will you come with us, Brista?"

After the briefest hesitation, she nodded.

It would have been faster to use the fourth tier.

Marra traveled the third. Because despite Tryst's return, despite the King himself saying the Trumen race was innocent, hostility still threaded through the Skullan people. Even the third tier now seemed treacherous - or perhaps some of those hostile stares she saw were in her mind.

When she entered the Agben School, Leah greeted her with a summons from Kirth.

The Skullan elder was out in the courtyard gardens, scraping algae that grew on the bottom of lily pads into glass vials. When Marra knelt beside her, Kirth handed her a vial and a slim knife. Carefully watching how the woman handled the water plant, she then imitated her movements.

Smells of peaty earth mixed with a mild tang, like a cabbage just a little too long cut from its bed.

"I believe you have sailed by ship before?"

Marra nodded.

"You shall do so again. We go on a long journey, you and I, to collect herbs. You will tell others only that we shall be gone a lengthy time."

"But Mistress..."

"They will assume we travel by land. Let them keep their assumption."

"Kirth, I cannot! Drail wishes me to travel with him."

At that the elder looked up. "Playing Brista to his band of gamesmen?"

Marra slowly nodded.

Kirth set the lily pad on the pond, careful to keep the top surface clear of water. Then she pushed herself up, with Marra leaping to assist.

When the elder was on her feet, she eyed Marra for several blinks of the sun before carrying three full vials to the drying shed.

Marra followed.

In the cool shade, the vials were set in the rack for today. All gathered plants would be placed there, and the wooden holder would be replaced with a new one that night.

"You missed studies because one man asked for

your help. Now you abandon school altogether because another beckons?"

"It's Drail!" Marra burst out. "He needs me."

"To make the same potion over and over for men who simply want the status of a Brista?"

Hot words leapt to Marra's lips - but she did not give them voice.

"Child, when will you follow your own heart?"

A sudden tear sprang to her eye. Heart tears, she heard her mother's voice. When something touched your soul, the moisture welled from deep within.

But she could not - must not - examine her feelings now. "I owe him a great deal," she told herself as much as Kirth.

"Seems to me," the elder replied, "that debt's been paid."

Drail thrust his mug high in the air. "To the Hand of Victory!"

All around the tavern table, the others did the same. Manten, his thick blond hair in a braid that Drail swore was never undone. Olver, who'd just cut his hair again, refusing for whatever reason to wear it long. And Fallon, whose answering smile was delayed.

Drail had intended to discuss the journey plans one more time. To see if Fallon could be prodded to join, or if anyone had a replacement idea. But the mood was far from serious, as victory tonight had been swift and dramatic.

And even as he pondered that, a Skullan entered the tavern.

Skullan were not unknown there. Indeed a group lounged in a corner, actually singing an old ballad with great enthusiasm though little skill. But this Skullan paused to scan the room before, with the barest nod at Drail, striding to the bar.

After a moment, Drail stood up to join him.

"That's good - another pitcher!" Olver pounded the table.

Drail signaled the barkeep as he stepped beside Jason, Tryst's Defense Master.

"You are summoned to the Palace," Jason spoke into his mug.

Drail bristled at the tone as much as the order. He said nothing, but Jason seemed to read his feeling.

"Please," he added, with a direct look and a tiny smile. "Tryst needs your insight."

After a moment, Drail nodded. "When?"

"Tomorrow after breakfast."

Jason downed his ale in a single tilt of his elbow, and left.

"Drail, of the Hand of Victory."

Tryst rose to stride across the council room, ignoring the wrath of his sire and grandsire, ignoring Minister Charis' surprise.

"Thank you for coming," he smiled.

He had his reward when Drail relaxed and grinned

back.

Tryst placed him in the empty chair beside his own. The council table had never been this full, he realized. And for the first time it felt right, useful. A council of men with experiences and wisdom in the thing to be discussed.

"Drail has played comet on two continents, against two races," he told them all. "The strategy differed greatly in the desert than here in Missea. This gamesman was able to recognize and adapt."

Drail eyed him warily.

"We have need to adapt again. To prepare a team to play on the Dim Continent."

His father and King Ganny had warned him to say no more. They didn't trust any Trumen, and this was a matter of security for the realm.

More, Drail owed no allegiance to the crown or the man.

But for some reason the journey intrigued the Trumen. His eyes sparkled with interest. "No one has ever played Terrin before."

Tryst caught Jason's surprised expression, and had to suppress a smile.

"You have reason to go there? An important one?"

"We do." Tryst felt the tension, the other men's concern that he'd say too much. But he knew there was no need.

"I'll go," Drail told them in that open, honest way of his. "I believe Old Merle, Manten, even Olver will do the same. Fallon...Fallon will not."

"I will be the fourth man," Tryst said.

"You'd do well to have a spare."

"I'm your spare," Jason rose to his feet.

Drail looked at him askance - Jason stood head and shoulders above the tall Trumen. "I'll slouch," the Defense Master shrugged.

The sparkle livened in the gamesman's eye. He nodded. "But we tell the Hand of Victory. So they can make a proper choice."

"They do not need to know," King Ganny barked.

Tryst's grandsire's bark had quailed weathered soldiers, but Drail stood firm. "They are men. Trumen, but men all the same. They have a right to decide whether to risk more than losing a game."

Tryst saw the dawn of respect in his grandsire's eye, before the argument began in earnest. Ganny was strong-willed; as was King Bactor. In the end, however, it was Tryst's will that prevailed. He would again assume the disguise of a Trumen gamesmen. And Jason, despite his size and his Skullan physique, would do the same.

Talking to Mauric in the garden later, Tryst nearly asked his friend as well. The boy had guessed something was in the wind and cajoled to be included. The temptation was hard to resist - Mauric's quick smile and lighthearted views had a way of warming the coldest of obligations. But this was no state visit.

Reading his decision, Mauric sighed. "How long will

you be gone?"

"Unknown," Tryst told him. "Perhaps a full cycle of seasons. Maybe more."

"I could..."

Mauric frowned at something behind him. Turning, Tryst saw Marra silently hurrying down a distant path. No doubt heading back to her school.

"Kendrick of Malle has been a stout champion," Mauric said. "Perhaps he's earned a fine palace chamber."

Tryst didn't see his point.

"If Marra doesn't want her garden room -"

"It's hers to do with as she will. Kendrick can sleep with his woman."

When Mauric gave him a speculative look, Tryst rose and strode off to seek Drail.

In the coming weeks Tryst grew determined in the plan.

He had the right men, he knew. In some ways Drail had trusted him with his team, his honor, even his life. It was a sobering burden, but he saw no better way.

His only real qualm came when Marra realized she was to be excluded. The Agben Women had indeed swept through the Palace, although he noticed Marra had not been among their number. When asked, Kirth informed him that Marra was not of a level to do such work.

Tryst wondered if the girl might be avoiding the

place after King Ganny's accusations.

So he went to a Trumen comet game. Their departure date was set, their passage booked, and he wished to take his leave of her before other priorities took over.

Entering the arena with Jason at his side, Tryst saw her standing by Drail. The gamesman frowned, but Marra welcomed him with a smile.

"I've come to say goodbye," he clasped her hand. "We leave soon, and will be gone for some time."

"Drail is also leaving," she told him. "We're traveling the continent to play comet."

Drail appeared as startled as he was.

"Oh, Marra...I never told you..." The Trumen seemed to ponder, before forcing a grin. "It's going to be a long journey. You should stay and finish your schooling."

"But you need me to go," she said slowly. Her voice was calm, but something in her face worried Tryst.

The gamesman hesitated, perhaps ready to concede. Tryst shook his head.

"Not this time, little one," Drail produced a smile. "We could be gone a long while."

The fleeting hurt on her face disturbed him, even after she smoothed her expression and nodded. She probably felt they were all abandoning her.

Tryst felt a pang of regret. For a blink of the sun he even considered bringing her, but this was far too dangerous. And, unfortunately, far too secret to tell her the truth.

The set of her mouth before she turned away would bother him later as they voyaged across the sea.

Marra watched the Hand of Victory win their game, though she barely saw the play. She smiled and nodded, wished Tryst good journey, and took the first opportunity to slip away.

Why had Drail changed his mind?

Something felt off in that. Tryst, she was sure, had known Drail would leave her behind. Odd that he, too, was traveling.

Entering the Agben grounds, she found herself racing up the spiral stairs to Kirth's room. So no one needed her anymore; the elder would say that was a good thing.

And Marra could go on her own journey - if Kirth would still have her.

Marra sat up in her berth, clutching the rim of the porthole to steady herself.

Something had woken her from a sound sleep. Peering through the glass, she could see a lightening sky outside, promising dawn to follow. The Rosy Lady's movement had smoothed, the rough pitching finally abated. It took a moment for her to realize what she saw.

As night cracked open with the dawn, Marra caught the vague outline of something high and wide and jagged.

Land, she realized. After four months at sea, they had found the Dim Continent.

She glanced back across the tiny room, where Kirth lay in her matching bed. The elder slept like always, both deep and peaceful. Marra marveled at her ability to do so. Of course, there was little else to do on the voyage; by comparison, traveling to Missea had been festive. Possibly because the Trafalcon had been twice as large. Or the gamesmen twice as lively.

If Kirth had been awake, she'd likely advise her to sleep now. But Marra had no intention of missing her first glimpse of a land she'd always thought myth.

So she rose and dressed.

Their cabin was two steps higher than the deck, with a single rope handrail strung down the center. And unlike handrails on land, Marra learned early on this one was necessary. The ship's rolling gait made it so.

Men - all Trumen - clambered high into the rigging, yanking lines and pulling sails. Already two of the canvas sheets had come down.

The First Mate appeared beside her, offering escort to the side rail. And she took it, for the same reason she held so tightly to the handrail.

On the Trafalcon, the lowering of sails meant arrival in port. They started long before docking, but usually with the city in sight. Now, however, Marra saw nothing but a solid wall of vegetation.

"We'll drop anchor just before breakfast," the First

Mate told the air before him and strode away. The Trumen sailors on the ship did not like to talk to Kirth. They were never openly rude, but they had a way of not seeing her - which in truth was not easy as the elder stood taller than any of them.

Already the sun was bright, with a warmth in the breeze found more often in the desert than Missea. This warmth was different though, with a heavy feel to the air. On the Flats where Marra grew up, moisture never accumulated on the body. The greedy sun would leech it too quickly off the skin. Indeed, if one grew clammy from perspiration it was a sure sign of illness.

In the past days as they neared land however, moisture had drenched everyone by mid-afternoon, the air here too full of water to hold any more. Marra couldn't wait to bathe on shore - there was only so much she could do with a small basin and a pitcher of salt water.

The breeze shifted, and she caught her first smells of the Dim Continent. Peaty, dense earth, and a sort of spice-grass, only more pungent. The odor of Kwitt - a horrible smell she'd experienced from the Terrin - was absent.

Breathing deeply, Marra released a tension deep in her shoulders she hadn't known was there.

And turned. It was time to wake Kirth.

Though Marra kept watch out the porthole, she never saw a hint of civilization. Not as Kirth dressed, not as the ship slowed to a crawl.

They dropped anchor with no dock in sight. The Crew set a gangplank down to the water and for a fleeting moment, Marra wondered if they meant to murder them.

Then the first mate assisted Kirth to the plank, hoisted both their satchels, and followed her down. Belatedly Marra hurried after them.

Kirth seemed to stand on the water.

It was only when Marra reached the end of the gangplank that she saw the three logs, lying side by side just beneath the timid waves. The elder was already trudging toward the wall of green leaves when the first mate offered Marra her belongings.

Wordlessly she took them and darted after Kirth.

She counted forty steps before an angry looking eel drove the number from her head. With a wide-eyed stare he shot off toward deeper water. The gentle sea lapping as high as mid-calf urged her on.

Marra felt dizzy watching the waters swirling past. The sandy bottom, with its seaweed and occasional fish appeared just below the surface, but she'd learned on Mid Isle that such transparency was misleading. The water could be over her head.

And being desert-born, she'd never learned to swim.

Kirth reached the verdant mass and disappeared. Marra trotted forward - to spy a narrow opening in the green curtain. Two sticks jutted through the vines, holding them apart. Marra hesitated only a blink of the sun before passing through.

It was dark within.

"Patience, Marra. You will soon see," Kirth said beside her.

Marra squeezed her eyes shut and counted to ten. When she opened them the shadows had retreated, revealing the earth rising steeply before her.

Kirth took a single step towards it and when Marra followed, the elder hurried on.

As they climbed, the light grew to mid-morning brightness though the slope remained steep. It was as a tunnel, not through dirt but through thick vegetation, and Marra could have gathered many plant samples merely by reaching out.

When a vine-colored rope appeared through the growth, Kirth used it as a handrail.

Overhead leaves thinned and then vanished. When Marra glanced over her shoulder, she saw the sea far below. It startled her how high they'd climbed.

Stairs appeared, flattened stone set in dark dirt with a peaty smell. Nutrients, Marra realized. The earth here was full of nutrients, much more than the Great Continent. That's why the plants grew so profusely.

Ahead, the elder dropped her hold on the rail as her stride changed. They had reached the summit.

Kirth passed through an arch into the sun. Marra followed.

They stood in a garden so carefully tended it could

almost rival those of Tryst's Palace. Almost. Green
carpet, trimmed low, walled by hedges, and a center
burst of scarlet flowers in three circles. But the scent
differed - more powerful, more peaty, and ladened
with spice.

Marra stooped to touch the grass - and found it was
not grass at all, but a moss that grew thicker and taller
than any she'd seen. It clung to a mixture of earth and
tiny stone.

"What is this?" she asked.

"Bray dust," a deep voice answered. She looked up
to see a deep green robe - silky and fine - flowing
round Terrin feet.

For a wild instant, she thought the creature from
the Palace had found them. But instead of grabbing
her, this one touched fingers with Kirth.

"Chance is kind to bring you to me once more, my
friend," the Terrin rumbled. Its fangs appeared longer
than ever - and she guessed that it was smiling.

"Marra, this is Tinge," Kirth grinned fondly. And
added, "Goodness child, stand up."

Marra did.

Tinge held out her paw. Kirth gestured impatiently,
and Marra brought herself to clasp it.

When she did so, she noticed the silver dove
pendent around its neck. Just like the one Leah had
first shown her.

"Bray dust," the Terrin repeated. "It cleans the feet
of dirt when you walk upon it. And augments any

mixture - locking the potency in to last a very long time. You can tell its use by the thickening of the potion."

"Agben!" Marra gasped. "You are Agben!"

Tinge's fangs grew long again. The Terrin's smile would take some getting used to.

Marra never would have found Tinge's house.

The path was clear enough. But the dwelling seemed more outdoor gathering place than home. They followed a short trail out of the garden, round a giant tree with a base wider than Marra was tall, and trod upon three stones carefully set in a meandering brook to reach the dwelling.

If dwelling it was. A large planked platform rose at the end of the path, shaded by a conical roof of tree branches tied together with green strands. Upright logs supported the roof, as the woven grass walls appeared incapable of doing so.

And most of those walls were only half-height, rising to Tinge's hip and Marra's shoulder, which left huge gaps between their top edge and the roof. It allowed much light inside - along with anything else that might care to wander in. There were more than a few insects on the path and in the garden.

The only inner wall sectioned off a small portion of the platform. The rest was laid bare to see - a sophisticated stove, benches tucked beneath a table ladened with food, and a second table crowded with glass vials and herb jars. On the far side squatted a gigantic bed and a scarlet rug surrounded by four large, white-cushioned chairs.

"Are you hungry?" Tinge asked.

Marra realized she was, having had no breakfast that morning. Cautiously she approached the table.

Kirth, eying her in amusement, snatched a dainty confection topped with white foam, and bit.

Tinge watched Marra expectantly.

As the elder took a second bite, Marra selected a cake - so moist that bits of it stuck to her fingers - and sampled it gingerly. It was tangy with flakes of sweet meat, topped with a buttery cream. Delicious.

"Coconut," Tinge purred. "My personal favorite."

Tinge chose a similar morsel and gracefully moved to a chair. Marra watched, fascinated, as the creature lowered itself. Its legs seemed so thin and fragile beneath the body mass.

Kirth followed, taking the seat beside it.

"I am very pleased to see you, my dear friend," Tinge rumbled. Marra stared at the green, upper jaw fangs that remained in full view during her speech. "But I did not expect to do so again. Where is our dear Rain?"

Kirth gestured, and Marra hurried over to climb into one of the large seats.

"That is a question I'd very much like answered," Kirth replied. "When was the last time you saw her?"

"At the appointed time, a year ago." Tinge eyed Marra closely. "Is little Marra here her replacement?"

Marra blinked.

"We shall decide, soon enough. What can you tell me about Rain?"

"She broke your dictates. But you know that."

Kirth inclined her head.

"She studied, that one. Everything I would teach her. I held back certain things, but she learned more in the interior."

Kirth was quiet for several blinks of the sun. Marra saw the elder's hand tremble before clasping the chair arm as if to calm her mind. "The interior?"

This time Marra had no trouble seeing Tinge's smile. "You thought that was one of our rules? Your mentor - no, her mentor - put that rule in place. We merely honored her and held our tongue."

"You didn't hold it with Rain."

Tinge rose to full height before walking back to the table for more treats. "Rain probed with many questions. I merely answered. Marra," the Terrin's eyes twinkled, and she no longer seemed terrifying. "Would you like another cake?"

Marra went to the table - to be sure the cake was still free of insects. And seeing that it was, she helped herself.

Tinge observed her careful perusal. "You worry about gnats, perhaps? All of your species does - but there is no need. They are repelled at the wall."

"How far did Rain travel?" Kirth asked.

"The first time she was gone maybe a handful of

days. She went farther each time - perhaps two moons at the end."

"The Tower?"

Tinge's fangs tilted up and down. Nodding, Marra realized.

"Most assuredly. I don't know how many times in all."

Drail strode down the dock.

Old Merle strode with him. Olver and Manten remained on the ship, sleeping off a large quantity of the barreled liquor the Captain had introduced them to the night before. And Tryst and Jason had headed in a different direction.

Even from the wharf, Creesby seemed an odd place. And while part of Drail resented this trip - resented being 'in service' yet again to the Skullan prince - part of him enjoyed the wonder of new places. The journey across the Wavering Continent to Port Leet had been an adventure, with new sights for the eye and people waiting to be discovered. He hadn't realized how much he missed it until now.

The Great Continent was home to the Skullan race, with the Trumen making up less than a third of the population and considered inferior. Here in Creesby Trumen dominated the harbor area overwhelmingly, yet there were Skullan about.

And from what he could tell, these Skullan lacked that superior attitude. When Tryst and Jason had first disembarked as Skullan, sailors made way for them exactly as they did for Drail, or any man not unloading cargo. There had been no deference paid to their race. As Drail reached the dirt street, a Trumen male strode past with all the confidence of his Skullan counterparts.

Creesby buildings were what he'd expected in Missea. Brick or wood walls, a sort of thatch in the roof. And while buildings rose two or even three levels high, no towering structures dwarfed the streets, no bridge-roads spanned high overhead. He would have thought it a large and prosperous city if he had never seen the Skullan capital.

Damp heat rose on his skin. Being desert born the heat didn't bother him, but air plump with water did. It would make comet that much more challenging.

A tavern with a white-washed front and two boys polishing the stoop caught his eye. He would have kept walking, but Old Merle turned and mounted the steps. It would be expensive, Drail knew, which was why he would have instinctively passed it by.

But expenses should not be a problem with the prince paying the bills. And Old Merle liked his comfort.

"We have rooms to spare," the barkeep beamed at them. "Four silver each for a night."

"Too high," Drail told Old Merle. In truth Tryst would not count cost - but he felt uncomfortable letting the barkeep know that.

Old Merle, sensing his thoughts, nodded and turned as if to leave.

"I can do a bit better if you be taking several rooms," the barkeep offered. "Or be taking several nights."

"How much better?"

They found themselves with four front rooms, large and sporting harbor views. Surely luxurious enough even for a prince, though Drail suspected Jason could yet find fault.

With accommodations secured, there was nothing to do but wait.

It was dark when Tryst found Drail and his gamesmen dining in the tavern.

His own task had been to find the gate - which proved easy - and discover how to pass through it - which proved difficult. Apparently while all of Creesby stood open and friendly, the rest of the continent was less welcoming.

Manten and Olver sat downing ale, recovered enough from the previous night's excesses to repeat the experience. Jason spun toward the bar, his hand yet again slipping up to touch his hair. The gesture was becoming a habit, one that would have to be broken quickly.

Having not shaved their heads for the length of the ocean journey, and dutifully plied an Agben tonic, they both sported hair a full hand and a half's length.

While Tryst found it irksome, Jason profoundly hated it.

In Missea he'd even produced wigs, in the hopes of keeping his own skull bare. Old Merle had guffawed long and loud while Drail shook his head. In the heat of a comet game, fake hair would be yanked free.

A scuffing of wood on wood woke Tryst from his musing, as Jason shoved a mug and a bowl of stew across the table toward him. The stew had a creamy spice base, with a high ratio of plant to meat. Tryst shouldn't have liked it - but he did.

The ale, in an odd stein with handles on either side, somehow cooled a spicy tongue.

"Well?" Old Merle prodded. Tryst realized that Drail had ceased asking questions, probably because they were never answered. He resolved to change that.

"They will send a guide," Tryst told them. "No later than two days."

Drail stirred. "Two days?"

Jason grimaced. "Apparently we must wait upon their convenience. I tried to find a second guide place, but it seems there is just the one."

As the Defense Master spoke, Tryst watched a girl stride through the door. Tall and blond, her short hair was a mass of wild curls untamed and proud. A long cape of vibrant green swung about her slim figure as she paused to survey the faces. Too short for a Skullan, yet her bearing did not seem that of a Trumen. Flinging back her cloak with a practiced gesture, the girl showed a confidence rarely seen in a female.

Then she locked eyes with Tryst - and approached.

Manten grinned. "You, lass, may warm my lap."

The blond looked him up and down. "I think your lap needs cooling." Turning to Tryst, she demanded, "Are you Jason?"

Jason, seated beside him, frowned. "Have you news of our guide?"

Whirling a nearby chair, the girl flung a leg over it in one smooth motion. She perched straddling the seat, and relaxed her arms along the backrest. "Good news. Your guide is here."

The others turned, scanning the room behind her. But Tryst had seen enough to guess the source of her arrogance. "You have guided others deep into the continent?"

"There is a lot of continent behind the gate," she told him. "I have seen more than most. I am Adeena."

"We do not want a woman," Drail said.

"Indeed you do," she smiled.

3.

MARRA AWOKE to the sound of birdsong. Her eyes blinked open to see the undulating jungle just six paces from her nose. She shot up on her pallet and remembered where she was.

The Terrin pallets Tinge had produced last night had indeed been more comfortable than she had imagined. Large and square, they consisted of similar stuffing to any mattress, except the surrounding 'bag' of cloth was missing. Somehow the herbal straw held together - and actually soothed rather than scratched the flesh. Marra had doubted that, despite Kirth's assurances.

It was the lack of finished walls that bothered her this morning. Traveling in the desert, she was used to sleeping out in the open, but the sparse landscape had never made her feel claustrophobic. Here thick vegetation crowded the space, smothering everything. The sheer vastness of the smells overwhelmed her.

Easing to her feet to don her skirt and blouse, Marra tiptoed past the sleeping Kirth.

On the other side of the jungle house, she found the door to the interior wall open and Tinge inside, busily working with vials and greenery. The Terrin's fangs lengthened into her smile, and Marra approached.

"Yute favors us with a pleasant morning, Marra," the creature rumbled. "Fetch me one green dish from the garden, if you will. They're set in the center of the flower circles."

Marra hurried to do her biding, only hesitating at the edge of the platform. She didn't relish stepping through the greenery without her shoes - but those were beside her mattress, and she might wake Kirth.

So she trotted out across the moss, and was delighted at the feel beneath her feet. The finest carpets lay in the Missea Palace, soft and thick and offering a tiny spring to the step, but this plant put the rugs to shame. It was like walking on a rare desert cloud.

Spying a green dish among the first flowers, she stretched out to retrieve it. The dish contained a sea of floating dots that bobbed gently with her gait. Seeds, she thought, and marveled at this method of gathering them.

She was still smiling when she handed the plate to Tinge. "How do you capture seeds in this manner?"

"They are not seeds," Tinge said as she poured the contents into a bubbling pot perched on the stove. Marra peered down, spying a few specks clinging to the dish edge. She leaned close as one of the specks moved.

It was an insect.

Jerking back, she stared at the Terrin. Tinge's fur quivered as she emitted a strange purr that kept interrupting itself, as if her throat were opening and closing on the sound.

Laughter.

"Skin women choose their components from but one spectrum of the world," she rumbled, stirring the pot with a forked stick. "We Terrin do not limit our choices to things with roots." Even as she spoke, Tinge reached for a wide mouth jar of feathery leaves and plucked the cork lid from it.

A powerful odor wafted through the air. "Kwitt," Marra gasped.

Tinge nodded. "How would you know Kwitt? Surely you've only seen it in a powdered form?"

Drawing closer, Marra nodded absently. The leaf was a single dark green stem with a hundred delicate threads attached, resembling a green feather. The threads looked fragile - and more potent than anything Marra had ever seen.

Her finger lifted to touch it.

"Have a care, little skin girl," Tinge rumbled. "Lacking the protection of fur on your paws, it is not...wise."

Marra pulled her hand back reluctantly.

She studied Tinge's table, with the long oval dishes in bright blue colors. There were three of them, stained with a dry dark residue. They, too, smelled of Kwitt - and something more subtle. A sort of - dark earth, and vaguely unpleasant.

Tinge continued her stirring.

Looking around the hut area, Marra noted again the wide openings to the jungle breeze. Impulsively she climbed atop a stool, and saw the bare, flat top of the wall.

She jumped down and darted outside, turning to study the house. Set in the wall, just beneath the opening, was a notched shelf - with a blue dish tucked inside. Marra sped around the platform, counting the notches. Twelve in all - and three were missing dishes.

She returned to stare up at the Terrin. "A bug repellent?" she asked, pointing at the bubbling pot.

Amused, the large creature purred again. "You lack fur but not wit, skin girl. Few living things would pass near such a brew."

"Kirth called Kwitt a mind relaxant. A powerful one."

"Relaxant? Interesting description. We call it a suppressant - tricks the mind into not thinking upon that which we wish to suppress."

"By the Desert Crane...you practice the third discipline," Marra whispered, more to herself than the Terrin. But Tinge chuckled all the same.

"We practice the art of crafting powders and potions to achieve goals," she declared. "Skin people fear the power unleashed, yet admit the value of the results. Thus they divide the art into disciplines, and cut an entire branch out of existence."

"But why?"

"Because that branch demands harm to living beings," Kirth spoke from behind. Marra whirled, to find the elder Skullan watching her sadly. "Because the results never justify the cost."

A wave of guilt passed through Marra - but on its tail came confusion. "Rain's bowls of pink gruel recognized Tryst." And as the words hung in the air, she gasped. "By using...*bits of him?*"

Tinge's eyes widened. "Recognized an individual skin man? Our Rain has indeed forged her own path."

Kirth laid a hand on Marra's arm. To silence her, she realized.

The Terrin picked up on Kirth's concern. "By Yute's own luck, I have only answered her questions," she said. "I did not seek to instruct your student. But she is smart, this one. More so even than Rain."

"Very smart," Kirth sighed. "But this one has some sense as well."

Marra doubted that. Because, she suddenly realized, she had just told a Terrin - the very race that had kidnapped a prince and a king - that they knew all about Rain's treachery.

It was two weeks before Tryst saw the other side of the gate.

First they had to formally apply to travel the continent, a thing not often allowed. King Ganny's suggestion to assume the role of Gamesmen proved wise, as the first demand was to know their destination. Tryst had thought once beyond the gate it wouldn't matter, but Adeena swiftly corrected that notion.

"Time beyond the gate is calculated," she said, her eyes piercing his. Trying to read his thoughts, no doubt. "Guides are required to provide estimates and routes before, and verification afterward. It is a crime to veer from your stated path."

Tryst found this impossible to believe. "With all that travel..."

"Few travel these days," she smiled. "Fewer still on their first visit to Creesby. Monitoring the gate is a well-paid responsibility. Now gate minders carefully count both days gone and skin men admitted."

"How do we estimate?" Jason demanded. "We are gamesmen, seeking to hone our skills. As we know nothing of what lies beyond the gate, how will you determine our path?"

Tryst saw the change in her, and realized King Ganny had called it right.

The girl studied Jason, and then each of the others in turn. "This thing you say is truth?"

Instinctively she looked to Tryst. He nodded.

For the first time she looked unsure. "I believe they will determine our first stop."

"You believe?"

Adeena nodded absently, as if still pondering the ramifications. "A place that will gladly enjoy your gamesmanship."

"And then?"

She met Tryst's eye. "If you measure well, I believe you can travel as you will. The normal restrictions will not be set."

Jason smiled. "And we won't need you."

The blond smiled back. "You will need me if you pass. The land is too...difficult for newcomers."

"Only if we pass?"

"If you fail, you will need a healer."

Having looked over - and disparaged - their gear, Adeena dragged Jason around Creesby to purchase sleep hammocks, pest repellents, and knee boots. Tryst expected his defense master to balk at new supplies, but Jason did not.

"There appears to be reason behind these," Jason told him across the tavern table.

"I've encountered sleep hammocks before," Tryst said, and grinned at his mentor's surprise. "I prefer my back against solid ground."

"Apparently there are places beyond the gate where you will not."

Adeena joined them, striding through the patrons with a proud tilt of her chin and a mug in her hand. She was too tall for a woman, Tryst thought. Too smug.

The guide joined them as Manten poured ale from the pitcher.

"Have a care what you drink tonight," she told them. "We pass through the Gate on the morrow's dawn."

"Let us wait till after breakfast," Olver clasped his mug.

"We go at the time appointed or wait for a new time to be given."

Olver muttered something under his breath. Tryst suspected it was both unflattering and overheard. Her reaction, however was faint amusement.

A confident woman, he thought to himself. As confident as the proudest Skullan female, though perhaps for different reasons. He wondered if she exaggerated the difficulties of passing through the Gate and traveling Terrin lands.

His doubts faded the next morning, when the entire party approached the stout bastion to be counted and questioned.

Still blinking the sleep from their eyes, the others stood in line to face the gigantic portal before them. Missea's gates had always been impressive, built to allow six wagons abreast to pass without difficulty.

This thing before them now rose just as high and wider still. He was curious to see how mere men opened it.

Four Trumen - he was pretty sure they were Trumen - met them. The tallest talked long to Adeena, taking her staff to study as the others circled the travelers.

"You are indeed Trumen?" one demanded.

Drail nodded once, bestowing such a look as to question the man's intelligence. Tryst turned to suppress his smile. Drail, he knew, wasn't acting at all. The gamesman took the question personally - and was insulted by it.

At last the gatekeeper stepped back and returned their guide's walking stick.

Then, fiddling with an odd knob, he opened a small doorway hidden within the massive gate. The same trick, Tryst realized, as the Palace used upon certain wrought iron gates. Allowing men to pass without going to the effort of swinging wide the huge portal itself. It also barred wagons or other conveyances from passage.

He noted the man counting again as each gamesman stepped through. Perhaps Terrin were as timid as the legends claimed.

Which made the treachery against the Skullan Empire all the more astonishing.

Stepping through the gate's tiny doorway, Drail

emerged onto well-tended flagstone.

Wide and undamaged, the road stretched out before them, offering new vistas and adventure. The main gate highway out of Missea was no more impressive - though surely more crowded. Here they were the only travelers, at least this morning.

This early in the day the heat had yet to thicken the breeze. Noises collided in the gap - the low buzzing of insects, rustling leaves as small animals scurried away. And, as the gate latch clicked shut and Jason marched away, light-pitched melodies trilled the air. Bird song.

Such noises occurred outside Missea of course, and could even be found in the desert. But to hear so many at once - Drail shook his head. King Ganny had spoken of a continent teeming with life. For the first time Drail wondered just what sort of life that might be. It was said not every creature on the Dim Continent ran from the sounds of men.

The Prince strode past. Drail matched his stride.

"Quite a road for such a lack of travelers," Tryst remarked.

"Recent maintenance done," Jason pointed to brush marks in the dirt.

"Why?" Drail frowned. It seemed a lot of effort for something not truly used.

"Anticipation of future needs." Tryst and Jason shared a grim look.

Adeena strode confidently on, unaware or uncaring of their delay. With little choice, they followed.

Marra helped in the garden by collecting the bray dust, which proved no easy feat. The moss, while plentiful, was also delicate. Taking a fine weave cloth, she lightly applied Honeysuckle dew to the surface, laid it flat on the ground, and lifted it gently by the corners. The fine dust was then brushed into a funnel bowl - a wide glass bowl with a funnel lid atop. It was painstaking work, all the more frustrating as she could hear maddening snippets of conversation from Tinge's room.

"Why are you so concerned?" Tinge's voice trickled through.

Marra paused to listen, but Kirth's answering grumble was too low to decipher.

It took ten trips and careful application of the brush to reach the quarter mark level in the bowl. In all that time she learned only that Kirth wished to do something, and Tinge stood in her way. Yet at lunch, sitting in the big chairs and spooning a delicate stew into their stomachs, the two friends laughed over Marra's mistake from her morning work. The problem with bray dust, she had discovered, was not collecting it, but transferring what was collected into the bowl. She'd left a sprinkling of powder on the table, the floor, and most definitely on her skirt.

"I'll be more careful this afternoon," Marra offered.

"This afternoon we should travel," Kirth said, shooting an annoyed look at the Terrin.

"It is simply sleep in the bag tonight and three nights more," Tinge murmured over her food. "Or spend this evening comfortably nestled in fragrant straw before three nights of bag sleep."

Though she said nothing, Marra gaped at Kirth.

"You," the elder told her, "will be the first Agben apprentice to see the inside of the Tower in...many years."

"Tower?"

"The Tower of Zaria."

They spent the afternoon assembling supplies. Tinge packed a large sack with odd-looking grain balls - traveling fodder, she called them. Kirth laid out three sleep bags, which resembled the sleep hammocks Marra had once experienced on Mid Isle. Yet the cloth here was solid material, a dark green that blended too well with the jungle. The island version had been stretch nets, and proved most comfortable.

She hoped these would prove the same.

Kirth smoothed the material out flat, then rolled it evenly around the stick before tying the loose strings to hold it in place.

When Marra was sent to pack their things, Tinge protested. "No need to burden ourselves with so much. You can clean your clothing at the Tower, if you are so fastidious."

"We do not know when we'll return," Kirth answered. And though Marra was still learning to read the Terrin's emotions, she did not doubt the creature was unhappy.

Kirth woke Marra just as the sun ventured over the Terrin house wall.

"A last civilized breakfast," she said. "And then we leave."

They nibbled coconut cakes and drank a robust tea tasting of peat and spice. "Sustaining," Tinge called it. Marra did not find the sweet pastries nourishing, and wondered if the Terrin took more sustenance from her tea than her food.

She didn't ask, of course.

As the sun rose high enough to color the world and the shadows retreated from the moss-grass, they gathered their backpacks and slung sleep bags over their shoulders. Tinge produced special boots, made not of leather but some sort of stiff weave cloth. The boots laced all the way up to the knees.

Strangest of all was the men's breeches, constructed to stretch over her legs. The material clung to her skin, a sort of soft cloud over the lower half of her body.

Marra had only gone without a skirt once in her life - when she disguised herself as a boy. This clothing wasn't seemly.

Kirth smiled at her recoil. "The Terrin outfit is necessary, child. Long skirts here will collect...things."

By the time she'd donned the odd leggings and tied the drawstring around her waist, the two Agben elders waited on the moss. They didn't so much as glance her way before tramping off into the wild.

And wild it was.

No clear path beckoned, as far as Marra could tell. One direction looked as forbidding as the next. Then Tinge turned, rambling toward two of the taller trees. She passed between.

The twin trees forced them through single file, and the terrain being both lush and thick, they never walked abreast again.

Growing up in the desert, Marra had found the Great Continent crowded with plant life. One could hardly take a step outside the Missea gates without stepping on something. Kirth had explained that the abundance of water made it so.

Here water thrived in the very air, in the damp breeze and clouds so ladened with it they failed to rise as high into the sky as they should. Plants grew atop plants, scrambling through the shadows in a mad climb for the sun. She couldn't take a step without rudely brushing against something.

Watching Tinge, she realized the Terrin simply thrust through it all, untroubled by any damage she may cause. Kirth merely followed in her wake, allowing Tinge's bulk to clear a path.

So Marra fell in line behind them.

Passing between the trees, she gasped aloud. Her Skullan mentor threw a quick look over her shoulder, then resumed her march. Perhaps the elder interpreted her expression, or was content to wait to ask. Or, quite possibly, she deemed it unimportant.

Marra was grateful either way. For at the moment smells overwhelmed her; smells of Kwitt and earth and spicy exotic...things. Aromas she'd only faintly caught at the school, or not at all. Wild, potent, peculiar. In truth she couldn't find the words to assemble her thoughts.

As the day wore on, she had leisure to work it out.

Kirth worried ceaselessly as she trudged behind Tinge.

She worried that Rain had done more damage than she'd previously thought. She worried that the Tower itself might be involved. Zaria would make a formidable enemy.

And she worried that this...plot...had taken years to evolve. Years to grow into the threat it was, without any of the wise women of Agben even suspecting. When this was over, they must make changes to prevent future threats.

Assuming they survived this one.

She heard a slight stumble, a tiny gasp. Marra was young and strong, so probably her mind had just wandered. That was the one danger - bringing this girl to Tinge. With no understanding of caution, with no concept of maintaining balance or the dangers of the third discipline, the herb girl's thirst for knowledge might well exceed her caution.

Yet Marra cared about others. A strong sense of what was right guided her choices. Her mistakes rose from youth, not intent.

Still, aware of the girl behind, Kirth was reminded of another time traipsing after Tinge through the trees, blithely trusting that the trailing apprentice would follow the proper path. That time had been years ago.

And that girl had been Rain.

The wide road wound between several hills, narrowing gradually. Jason noted the evenly-set stones became less so as the plant growth between disturbed the base. Maintenance, he suspected, tapered off rapidly with the distance from the gate.

The similarity to Missea also tapered off. Seemingly normal grass now sported other plants with a bluish tinge, and the looming trees were too squat and close together. Each step shifted them farther from the familiar to the unknown.

Into the Dim Continent.

Adeena matched her steps to his. "You are the path minder?"

"I...pardon?"

"The path minder." She studied his face. "The leader drives the venture, having a goal in mind. He finds a path minder to keep them to the path. Such men see to the details, often are paid. They are not distracted by the leader's belief."

She probably thought she'd complimented him. "I believe in their...venture," he ground out.

The girl guide sent another penetrating look. "Then you do not mind the path. You mind the man."

"Jason," Tryst beckoned.

Adeena's lips twitched.

Having just crested the steepest hill yet, the Prince stared down at the fork in the road. It split three ways, one heading due east, one heading due west, and one continuing straight as an arrow. While the two sharp turns continued on through similar hills, the straight route vanished into a vine-threaded forest so thick the sun itself faltered in penetrating it.

"What do we do when we reach the bottom?" Old Merle eyed the girl.

Adeena carelessly pointed, already trotting downhill. "We travel straight, into the swamp forest."

Jason exchanged a look with Tryst. "Swamp forest?"

"Your first game plays out in Krum," she tossed over her shoulder. "The village lies in that direction."

Drail peered at Adeena's face suspiciously.

He'd watched her stride confidently down the embankment, eyes straight ahead, chin lifted. Almost too confident.

Then she called a halt at the edge of the trees. Something in her voice caught his attention, something he hadn't expected. Watching her eyes dart from the tree line to her feet, observing the squaring of her shoulders, confirmed it.

She was nervous.

Most women grew nervous at the slightest cause. When he first met Marra she frequently seemed so - in fact one of the things he admired was her courage to proceed anyway. Adeena, however, had all the confidence found in a man.

Even now she covered it, pretending she felt no different. But after playing comet for most of his life, learning to read opponents to know who was scared and who was brave, Drail knew the signs.

"What exactly is a swamp forest?" he asked.

"You're about to find out."

"You don't know either."

The look she sent was penetrating - and revealing. Seeing it, Drail spoke so the others couldn't hear. "I thought you'd done this before."

"I have!" she hissed.

He waited, letting the weight of silence drag the truth from her.

"Always to the right," she sighed. "My stick carries forty notches, and every one of them took the right fork."

For the first time Drail saw the marks in her staff.

"Why would our journey be any different?"

"You are my first gamesmen," she said, before turning to face the others. "We should eat before venturing inside."

"I thought," Jason frowned, "you merely guided our

steps. I thought we chose such times."

"Choose away," she turned back to the swamp forest. "It's dark in there, and difficult walking. There won't be convenient pause points for food or rest."

"How long through the forest?" Old Merle asked.

Adeena shrugged. "At your slow pace, Gamesman, it's hard to say."

Drail suppressed a grin. If he hadn't known otherwise, he'd never have guessed she hadn't traveled it many times before.

So they sat and munched hard cake, a specialty Adeena had provided in several bags. The small biscuits proved very tough to chew and tasted nothing like cake. Adeena deemed them both sustenance and portable.

"These things taste like hay muck-raked from a barn," Olver told her.

"And he would know," Manten grinned. Olver threw a piece at his friend's nose.

"If they were sweeter on the tongue, you'd be tempted to eat more than you need," Adeena said. "Their function is to provide the necessary nourishment to journey."

The sun burst free of a cloud, cheering Drail with its blast of desert warmth. It was both hot and humid here, but the heat at least was an old familiar friend. Lifting his face in welcome, he was yet aware of the ominous trees. "How long to our game?" he asked, eyes still closed.

A brief hesitation, and then he heard her sigh. "Three days, on average."

"On average?" Jason's sharp tone forced Drail to open his eyes.

Adeena shrugged - a gesture she frequently used to communicate. This one indicated a sort of apology. "Guides share all information, especially travel time. But some paths vary widely on that point - and this one more than most."

Jason was not happy with the answer - nor indeed was anyone else. Adeena herself showed a widening crack in her confidence.

Olver stirred, ready to fire a nasty retort.

"Then we'll discover it together," Drail smiled.

Stymied, Olver gave him a penetrating look before stuffing the last of his hard cake between his teeth.

Tryst watched their guide scan the tree line. "The entrance seems to be there," he pointed.

Adeena glared over her shoulder, before reaching into a fat bush. She plucked out a rounded twig - no, two twigs mated together. Tossing it on the ground, she reached for more.

Jason strode over to examine the thing. He was still frowning when he held it out to Tryst.

Two stout sticks, bound together at the either end, with a shorter stick forcing them apart in the center. Strips of cloth dangled from the edges.

Adeena tossed more of the things out, paused to

count, and then tossed a handful more. Fourteen in all, Tryst noted. Two for each in their party.

Selecting her pair, the girl sat on the grass to tie the things to her feet.

"You're playing a prank," Manten accused.

"Why?" Jason expostulated.

Her lips twisted as she tested the knots. "Yute's own luck! This is hard enough without having to justify every step of the journey. Put the bleeding things on...you'll find out why soon enough."

To Tryst's amusement, the men all did precisely as she bid.

Grumbling as they stood, glaring as they approached the entrance, he doubted the others saw what he saw. Adeena hesitated at the forest threshold, lifting a hand to the air before her. Her fingers stabbed at a single point, snatching back as if she'd caught an insect flying past. But he had seen no insect.

Holding it for a blink of the sun, she then pulled the fist to her heart, head bowing, eyes closed. He'd never seen such a gesture. Her...reverence...approached that of an elder Tower priest seeking the guidance of the Constellations.

Before he could even form a question, she marched off into the trees.

They followed.

Walking with the things tied to their feet proved difficult. The pointed bit at the heel stuck in the dirt, scraping out as the rest of the foot pushed on to the ground. The dense trees added to the challenge, blanketing the uneven ground in shadows. Presumably their eyes would adjust to the dark, though they hadn't yet.

A profound silence blanketed them as well. The very forest seemed to muffle the normal sounds one took for granted in the day. He didn't like it at all.

"What sort of animals dwell here?" Tryst asked, and winced at the loudness of his own voice.

"Animals?" Manten clawed at a leafy branch in his face.

"Predators," Jason told him. When Adeena hesitated, the Defense Master sent Tryst a needle-sharp look.

The guide lifted her foot, stepping up onto a thick carpet of...vines. Vines with rope-like stems tangling chaotically, the tiny leaves quivering at their passing. Adeena carefully trod three steps more before turning. "Above the platt, mostly harmless things dwell."

"Above the platt!" Olver stared down at their feet. "You mean animals scurry beneath this ugly thing?"

"Surely they couldn't be very big creatures," Manten frowned.

Adeena considered them, lips pursed. And then she leaned over the nearest bent tree trunk, twisting a piece of knotted bark free. She advanced three steps, pausing over a black hole in the platt. Eying them all, she dangled the bark over the void - and let go.

The thing splashed hollowly, as if dropped in a

puddle thick with mud.

"There are snakes all around, and darop - which look like logs and have large teeth - swim below. Some snakes are poisonous, but all will run or hide. They'll only bite if cornered. Darop will bite for no reason at all."

"Great Goose guide us!" Olver muttered. Adeena merely resumed her walk.

With the others hesitating, Drail stepped up on the higher level first, swaying slightly. "It's a bit unsteady," he warned.

Jason followed. Tryst made himself walk lest the others see his hesitation.

It wasn't enough to carry sleep-slings, forced to sway as they slept in unfriendly terrain. Now they traveled across a giant sleep-sling, suspended above even more unfriendly creatures.

He could almost hear Marra's sigh, calm and quiet in the shadowed wood. She'd square her shoulders in that manner of hers, and follow Adeena without a protest. Accepting it had to be done, and that was that.

He missed Marra, he realized. He missed her practical attitude, her acceptance of what fell across their path with nary a complaint. Stars, she'd probably stoop to gather plant leaves.

At least she was safe in Missea.

As the journey wound through the jungles of the Dim Continent, Marra's apprehension melted beneath the sheer abundance of plant-life.

The air shimmered with scents rich in potency and power. Her fingers touched fibers both velvet soft and hard shell-cased, some even with thorny protection. And with Kirth's approval, she collected as many as her two sashes would hold.

One tiny white leaf - for it was not a flower after all - smelled so good she had to suppress the urge to chew it. Strong aroma of cinnamon and vanilla made her mouth water, and beneath that lay a pleasant earthy aroma complimenting the pair. She tossed out a lesser specimen to keep a sample.

When Tinge bent low beside her, Marra gasped at the long string of glass vials dangling from her waist. They clicked against each other merrily.

A Terrin sash all of glass! How extravagant - and how wonderful.

Kirth observed her delight. "It takes years to learn how to move with a Terrin sash," the elder told her. "If the vials collide with any force they shatter. The only way for 'skins' to avoid that is to set them far apart, reducing the number you can carry. For us it's impractical." At Marra's frown, she added, "Terrin tread more carefully."

Tinge met her startled gaze with a long-fanged grin. "Or have thicker waists. Marra's found Elderbath," she added happily. "A powerful tea - very hard to find. By Yute's own luck - how did you see it in the foliage?"

Startled, Marra wondered that the Terrin couldn't

smell it, and glanced at Kirth.

"As best as we can determine, Terrin lack the ability to detect odor," Kirth told her. Tinge's fangs lengthened again as she nodded.

That night they employed the sleep bags. The Terrin contraptions used enough material that the edges folded completely around, tucking them away from the world. Tinge said it made sleeping easier, but Marra felt isolated. She didn't get a good night's rest until the second night.

Finally, waking refreshed, she enjoyed the morning's journey. They spoke of proper bases for potions as they gathered plants, as the path lead them up out of the trees. At a rocky ledge near the top of the climb, they munched grain balls - which were filling if bland - on a granite perch overlooking the ocean.

"We follow the sea," Marra said, surprised.

"The Tower lies within reach of the water," Kirth told her. "Zaria sends its people here, just as Agben."

Licking her furry fingers delicately, Tinge sent Kirth a swift glance. "Did Rain tell you as much?"

Kirth shook her head, and the Terrin purred with laughter. "You see well, my friend."

"I see belatedly," the elder sighed. "Can you not enter the Tower with us? Your understanding would be most useful."

Marra saw the quiver of fur, realizing Tinge was imitating Kirth's head shake. "Terrin culture is different from that of Skins. We keep...separate."

"You all live alone?" Marra asked.

Tinge stood, slowly moving her hips in the gesture she used whenever rising from a long sit. "Males dwell together, feeling their strength in numbers. Females may form an enclave or live alone, to suit our whim."

Marra saw her own confusion reflected in Kirth's face. "But what about children?"

Tinge lifted her backpack, settling it in place. "Terrin breed much as you. When a female's birth-time nears, she seeks a knowledgeable enclave. She can then stay to tend the offspring, or return to her old home."

Marra assisted Kirth to rise.

"At the age of bone shift, the young Terrin sets foot to a path of its choice. Males may seek the father, or another male dwelling. Females choose as well, even to finding an instructor of Agben or other skills. They may even decide to live alone for a time."

"So females are freer?" The words burst off Marra's tongue before she could stop them.

Tinge's rumbling laughter shook her whole frame. "By Yute's own luck, we are indeed," she finally answered. "But few males possess the wit to perceive that."

The Terrin lead them along the rock edge, climbing higher above the sea.

"But...how do you...?" Kirth's voice died. Belatedly, Marra guessed, realizing the impertinence of her question.

Either Tinge didn't think so, or didn't mind. "When a female wishes to breed, she approaches a male dwelling."

More questions rose in Marra's mind, but she didn't dare express them.

"That is why," Tinge's purring laugh threaded her words, "I cannot be seen at the Tower."

They journeyed three days more.

On the last day the rock ledge they followed darkened. Up early, Marra rubbed her hand across it, amazed at its glossy look and smooth feel. Like the black arena, she thought.

Still in her sleep-sling, the Terrin saw her and spoke. "Beware the rain on such a surface. The stone turns slick and dangerous to tread."

The black ledge continued, widening where they ate their noon meal.

When they finished the grain balls, Tinge set them to a jungle path winding down to a valley, and then up the other side. Trees grew thicker, shrouding them to the point where Marra could see only a few feet before her.

And then the path climbed and the trees pulled away to reveal the Black Tower.

Built of stacked stone, it rose two stories high and no wider than a Port Leet Tavern. Large perhaps by desert standards, but compared to Missean structures it was puny. This was the single presence of Zaria on the Dim Continent?

Kirth frowned, and Marra wondered if she too was startled.

Tinge led them right up to the wooden door - a simple, humble portal such as might be found on a desert home. The Terrin placed herself against the wall beside the hinges, where she would be hidden once it swung open.

Exchanging a look with Marra, Kirth knocked.

They waited.

Three blinks of the sun later, the door swung wide to reveal a tiny Terrin in a white robe. Startled, he clung to the door until an identical Terrin shoved him aside. This one's fangs lengthened in the smiling gesture.

"Chance has led your footsteps to the Tower of Zaria," he said. "Welcome, friends of Rain."

Kirth sucked in her breath. Before she could do more, Tinge popped around the door, eyes glittering angrily. At least Marra thought it was anger.

The smiling Terrin fell back as a spasm raced along his fur. Slowly he retreated inside as Tinge followed. When Kirth also passed into the dark, Marra cautiously entered.

But she left the door open. Just in case.

Growing up in the desert, Marra knew little of the Zaria Tower. Vague rumors barely percolated to the Flats of Beard, and those that did sounded more like folk tales than truth. Missea's stories were more detailed and more plentiful.

The Tower's interior startled her, for instead of the reputed richness of the priests, elegant objects and bejeweled tools, they found dirt, rough benches, and a table propped upon shaky legs. Lacking windows, the only light came from three sconces burning on the walls. Burning, Marra was certain, rag-oil - the cheap, diluted oil Misseans reserved for servant areas.

When Tinge finished her perusal, she snorted disdainfully and marched up the ramp of three rough logs to the second floor. The robed Terrin trailed behind, looking terribly nervous.

Kirth nudged Marra, pointing to the table top crusted with dirt. The whole place looked filthy and smelled stale. Tinge's open-air abode had been meticulously clean.

They followed the others up to the second floor.

Here a large window looked out upon the path they'd taken. Daylight streamed in upon two bedrolls hastily abandoned. A small table and bench stood by a row of shelves stacked with scrolls.

"Where is the priest?" Tinge demanded.

Marra gasped.

"These are acolytes," Kirth explained. "A Zaria priest wears red."

One of the acolytes swallowed before speaking. "He has been called..." his speech withered at Kirth's sniff.

"Has he?" Tinge growled. "And what are your instructions?"

Marra could hardly credit the fear she sensed in the two. Zaria, she always believed, scared others - yet these two cowered before Tinge. Was that because she was Agben or female?

"What do you know of Rain?" Kirth demanded.

With saliva dripping from his fangs, the first spoke up. "She is the most powerful of Agben. She will send others."

Tinge snorted and strode to the shelf, snatching and opening a scroll. When Kirth joined her, the two read. Marra watched the elder's lips thin in a manner that would have sent many a student scurrying out the door.

"The war foretold in the scrolls is now upon us," Tinge read aloud. "Your task is to remain here, safe from peril. We will return when the Trumen are gone".

"Gone?" Marra asked.

Kirth grabbed another scroll, scanned it and tossed it aside before grabbing another. And another.

"They're all the same." She flung the last one on the table. It curled tightly, rolled to the edge, and dropped off.

"I don't understand," Marra stared as the scroll struck the floor in a puff of dust.

"The third race war," Kirth spoke softly even as her hands clenched at her sides. "It seems Rain has taken a hand in prophecy."

Kirth followed Tinge back down to the acolytes' tiny kitchen, where a barrel brimming in grain balls squatted on the floor. Solemnly, the Terrin replenished her bag; Kirth beckoned little Marra to do the same.

"Where exactly do we travel to now?" Kirth prodded.

"The Tower of Zaria," Tinge answered.

"I thought this was the Tower," Marra paused with a handful of food.

"This was always a shill for the Zaria skins," Tinge replied. "The true Tower will take the better part of a moon's cycle to reach."

Words bubbled upon Kirth's tongue, threatening to boil over. Not trusting herself to speak, she firmly held them in check. For so long she'd been comfortable in her knowledge of Agben, of Terrin. She'd known her peers well, understood the subtle differences to be found on the Dim Continent.

Tinge herself had brought Kirth to this Tower ages ago, when she'd been young and eager to learn. For years when anyone spoke of the great Tower of Zaria, Kirth had inwardly smiled, knowing that the stories of opulence cherished by the Skullan were but myths. Now it seemed the true myth was Kirth's ever being allowed near the Tower at all.

Rain had kidnapped a prince and a king, all the while scattering her regal commands at the school. Fenna had been involved - perhaps even Britta.

And now she knew Tinge had lied to her.

When the Terrin lead them outside, onto a new path leading away from the sea, Kirth wondered just how many lies yet remained to be found.

And would she find them all?

4.

OR FOUR DAYS they traveled through the swamp forest. To Drail it seemed twice as long. With the enveloping hush of the wet wood and the tension of his companions, conversation died even as it was born. He kept himself on high alert, as the Defense Master called it, intending to see the snake - or darop - before it saw him. But the dark interior and continual muffled squish from their odd shoes against the platt dulled the senses.

Sitting in the fancy Missean palace, he'd thrilled at the idea of playing comet against Terrin. The ultimate challenge, exceeding even his grandsire's accomplishments. He'd blithely accepted.

Now, sleeping in dangling bags that cut him off from the air, walking on spread-shoes to keep from falling through leaf into darop-infested water, he suddenly recalled the size and strength of the only Terrin he'd ever glimpsed. The image wasn't encouraging.

His first Missean dose of reality, of facing a genuine Skullan team with all the mass and strength of the ruling race, had almost killed his dream. Beyond their size, Drail had confronted a whole new strategy to the game. Only determination, hard work, and coaching from an elite Skullan allowed the Hand of Victory to eventually climb back into the arena.

And he'd never truly succeeded, he reminded himself. He had yet to face a competitive Skullan team and win. Yet here he was, naively ignoring that fact in a quest to challenge creatures much more powerful. He'd never seen them play, had no idea about their twists to the game. And it was doubtful he'd find a Terrin mentor.

They encountered two snakes along their path. One they heard through its rasping hiss, but never actually saw. The other, when Drail brushed thick vines aside, suddenly appeared across his palm. With a yelp he'd flung the thing away.

Adeena pronounced both harmless, though she'd not seen either. No one questioned her call.

On the third day he chewed his hard cake lunch as he walked. Sitting while they ate had proved impossible, as rocks or fallen trees to sit upon were rare, and the hoard of insects inhabiting the platt made standing still unpleasant.

Drail's legs ached from the effort of traveling with the things tied on his feet. He could only hope they'd have time to recover before playing an actual game.

Adeena trudged just ahead of him, and despite all his concerns he found himself smiling. The guide was as tired as any of them, but stubbornly refused to show it. The telltale squaring of her shoulders appeared more frequently, and she no longer looked back to gauge their stamina. He suspected this last was to deny them the chance to gauge hers.

When she stopped abruptly, Drail swiftly stepped beside her.

Ignoring him, the girl inserted her hands into a particularly dense veil of vines, and pulled them apart.

Sunlight burst through. Gratefully they emerged from the platt.

The mood lightened as the sun warmed a countryside furred with shrubs and trees. Now the expedition could walk abreast. Manten made a ribald comment and even the Defense Master laughed.

Adeena said nothing, but he saw her shoulders relax as she knelt to untie her spread-shoes. He quickly did the same.

Shoes stowed - apparently lots of these were kept at the entrances to the jungle - Adeena suggested a break before moving on. They did not, however. Supposedly the Terrin village was near, and Jason urged no more delay.

Drail agreed. Not from eagerness to see the village, but a need to distance themselves from the swamp forest.

Tryst's relief was short-lived.

As the girl led them up a winding path, a tree at the crest of the hill moved. No, not a tree. A Terrin.

It balefully watched them with eyes glittering above green-tinged fangs. Covered in fur, the creature looked more like an upright bear than a civilized being. And though the elevated angle made height hard to judge, the watcher looked enormous.

Remembering the Terrin in the Black Arena, he knew the impression accurate.

Tryst had known this plan meant playing comet again, but in a vague echo to the dangerous whole. Now, with the monster looming, he realized the possible carnage in battling Terrin on the field. Visions of Port Leet games flashed, of young Kayle's injury and his own nervousness before playing. Stars, how big the Skullan must have seemed to Drail and his friends - how formidable, how dangerous. And here they blithely trotted into a whole new level of danger.

Adeena strode on to mount a tier of log steps and stand level to the waiting Terrin. The top of her head barely reached past its belly.

Its eyes fastened on the men. "What chance led you here?" it growled.

Someone behind him gasped. Tryst remembered Jason had not seen a Terrin this close.

"A lucky path of intention," Adeena spoke firmly.

The creature silently assessed their party for a handful of blinks of the sun. Then the fangs tilted, hopefully in a Terrin nod.

Adeena beckoned them to join her. They climbed the steps.

The Defense Master's head reached a level between the thing's breast and shoulder. His Skullan body appeared a twig beside a full grown tree. Observing him balefully, the Terrin's twin fangs glistened though the hair hid its lips.

Adeena solemnly bowed and with a flourishing gesture, stepped aside. "I present the gamesmen of the Hand of Victory."

Seeing the startled faces of his companions and the Terrin's unreadable reaction, Tryst clamped down a wild desire to laugh.

When Drail was a boy playing his first comet games, Raston taught him a trick.

The other boys, larger and with muscles more developed, would glare down at him, making all his confidence vanish in a blink of the sun. He lost those early games. His grandsire told him to look not at their eyes but at their movements. Observe tendencies and weaknesses - that was the way to win.

Now Drail calmly observed the village as they

walked, allowing himself to see it objectively rather than feel fear.

First impressions reminded him of temporary arenas, such as found in the Flats of Beard. Numerous platforms littered the area - with no sign of long standing buildings. On closer examination, however, these platforms appeared solid and well-crafted.

And they had roofs.

As their party strode through the center of a larger structure, he recognized a huge kitchen with stone fireplaces, kettles, and presumably dinner vegetables being sliced on massive tables. Such tables lined the central platform, those surrounded by giant chairs. Tables of lesser height filled the remaining space, with square mats replacing the chairs - presumably to sit upon.

The gathering hall and dining room.

Smaller buildings appeared to be work areas, where hairy inhabitants whittled wood and shaped metal utensils. These artisans paused to watch them pass, and did not resume their task.

Farther on clustered a sea of small platforms, with woven vine walls on two sides. For privacy, he decided. Glimpses of colorful dangling cloth suggested sleep slings.

Sensing Manten beside him, Drail turned to confront his friend's gaping mouth. Glancing at the others, he saw the same astonishment, the same nervousness echoed on face after face. His friends, he realized, had never been taught Raston's trick.

Drail threw back his head and laughed.

Adeena watched the gamesman laugh, his thick braid flopping with the gesture. Foolish, stupid.

Fearless. Yute's own luck, she admired him.

Other skins had come, declaring themselves gamesmen. All expressed interest in playing across the Dim Continent, though few ever ventured beyond the gate. Although she herself had never led such a group, she'd sat at the campfire and heard the tales spun by other guides. Few games had ever been played. When an ignorant skin saw his first Terrin, actually stood beside him to stare upwards like a small child at a grown man, courage vanished as a whisper wing in the mist. Reactions ranged from disbelief to terror.

Never laughter.

She recognized Drail's laugh, of course. It was defiance at the whim of Eutykia, the goddess of chance. An acknowledgment of Yute - the affectionate short name - setting a tough dinner table, and an affirmation that one would eat all the same.

Drail was proving to be something rarely seen off the ships from the Great Continent. A real man.

Smiling at him, she strode on behind the solemn creature that led the way. Taking them up the path to the Terrin with the red glow about his head. The glow, she knew, was from ashbark powder, in the red tint marking the Leader.

The Leader studied the group as the guiding Terrin growled a single word. "Gamesmen."

Adeena had dealt with many Terrin in her guide years and grown accustomed to their peculiarities. So it startled her when the Right Hand - the Terrin who served the leader - escorted them toward the circle in the moss.

He must be Right Hand. No other would dare do so.

Drail and the others stood where indicated, confusion shading their faces. Apparently these gamesmen didn't recognize the field.

"Comet," she said, and waved her hand.

Drail's brows rose as he grasped her meaning.

"This is an arena?"

"A comet field," she corrected. The fields in Creesby were all dirt, marked by the line where grass was allowed to grow. Here the entire field was the moss carpet Terrin liked. The boundary was more mystery than demarcation. Perhaps the fields in Missea differed even more.

"We play here? Now?" the one called Olver burst out.

"So it seems."

The skin men exchanged long looks.

Drail stepped away, bending to touch the moss before stretching his legs wide. With a shrug and a grin, he began warming up in a ritual sequence of muscle movements. The others slowly followed his lead.

Old Merle moved beside her. "Where are the opponents?"

Adeena pointed to the skin men emerging across the field. The old man stood close enough she felt his start. "Those aren't Terrin."

She blinked in surprise. "Did you think to play Terrin?"

A full five blinks of the sun passed. And then Drail burst out laughing once more.

Tryst watched the Right Hand approach.

A telling title, he mused. It indicated the creatures were right and left handed, like Skullan and Trumen.

The thing moved with a loping gait, as if the knees struggled with smaller motions. Catching Jason's steady gaze, he saw the Defense Master found the Terrin movement inferior, giving the 'skins' an advantage. But then Jason never saw the speed of the Terrin in the Black Arena.

Much could be learned by watching the creatures play comet. But then, they might be too busy trying to survive to actually observe.

Two Terrin carried an odd looking ring of points to field center, maneuvering it round the hairy lump in the middle - the cone, he realized. This comet cone was larger than those used in Missea, and somehow covered in fur. And the center circle, the perimeter that no player was allowed to cross without the judge's permission, was a circle of animal tusks, pointing outward to impale any who came too close.

By the Great Goose, did they cannibalize their own kind for a mere game?

Another Terrin followed, bearing a pail and a clutch of long...what appeared to be feathers. Those he dipped in the pail, and then brushed over the circled tusks.

"Do not go near that circle," Tryst said aloud. Manten and Olver exchanged a startled look.

Adeena frowned at them. "Of course you do not."

"Are those Terrin fangs?" Tryst demanded sotto voce.

"Those are darop teeth."

"Darop? Those things we walked over in the swamp jungle?" Olver spluttered.

The girl nodded.

"Stars," Olver whispered.

A Terrin with a yellow glow around his head loped out across the field. One of the men - Trumen, surely - strode out to meet him.

"Go," Adeena nodded.

"But there's only two teams."

The guide scoffed. "Challenge enough for you."

Still frowning, Drail trotted away.

"Are there other dangers?" Jason demanded.

Adeena's face revealed incomprehension. "Besides darops?"

Tryst sighed.

Long ago he'd woke in a strange land with strange customs. The most treacherous times came when he thought himself on familiar territory, only to realize he was not. To request a favored food, to find the name meant something different there. Or walk on a ship to sail home, to discover an expensive mark of health was required.

Here they stood about to play what should be a most familiar game. What price their ignorance now?

Poised at the edge of the field, Drail felt himself more in a dream than awake. Dark moss instead of sand beneath his feet, a dead predator's teeth where the cone should be. Proportions all wrong, with such a vast play area, large comet balls, and larger spectators.

Far larger spectators.

The judge's head glowed yellow as he beckoned, four balls at his feet. He stood far from field center, though Drail realized the center was too well guarded by fangs to stand there. Stars, this felt odd.

He trotted across the soft carpet, testing its slippery properties. They ought to practice a day before playing in such a different environment. They ought to practice an entire moon.

To his surprise, the moss covering gripped his feet more surely than sand.

As the other team captain approached, Drail noticed the man's team spreading out onto the field, drawing closer. He threw a quick glance over his shoulder, hoping Manten assembled the Hand of Victory.

"I'm Bran," the captain said, grinning like a boy about to play games with his friends.

"Drail."

The Terrin judge grew impatient. Or perhaps merely wanted his dinner. "Choose," he growled.

The captain - Bran - lifted a hand, hesitated. Drail bent to snatch his ball.

And rising again, caught Bran's stabbing gesture, snatching at air, then pulling fist to heart. The man's head was bowed as if standing before a Tower of Zaria.

He then grabbed a ball.

The Terrin raised paw to air. Drail watched, fascinated to see if a similar gesture followed. Thus he was caught off guard.

"Comet!"

Bran spun, shooting his comet towards his already running team. Drail glimpsed one man racing towards the cone before he whirled to his own men.

Lagging only slightly behind, Olver sprinted toward him while Manten peeled off toward the cone. Passing his ball to Olver, Drail continued his turn to see Manten angling to guard the ring of teeth from Bran's teammate.

The man threw the ball toward the cone yelling, "YUTE!"

After competing in Missea for so long, Drail found himself gaping. Comet was won by sinking a high value ball, and not necessarily first. Skullan played for time, allowing the soot covering to wear off and reveal the number of dots beneath. Thus knowing the value of the ball before they sank it.

It seemed a different strategy prevailed on the Dim Continent.

Fortunately Manten's instincts sent him diving between gamesman and cone, leaping to catch the ball, rolling across the moss and back onto his feet.

He launched the sphere from twenty paces away - straight into the cone. Olver's ball sank a blink of the sun later, though Olver was much closer. The other team ceased.

Silence reigned - before the Terrin roared.

Drail turned slowly, fearing attack. The hairy things leapt into the air, crying battle words and other shrieks he didn't know. But they remained in place and off the field.

Bran trotted to him, the man's astonishment giving way to another grin.

"Yute - that was well done! You Missean types usually waste time being afraid to take your shot."

Pounding his shoulder, Bran led him off the mossy field.

Tryst had been to many celebratory feasts, including a few for dignitaries with bizarre customs. This feast would raise that mark to a whole new level.

To begin with, Terrin ate only vegetables. They

roasted thick roots over a center fire built to blaze in a low, wide circle. They dipped fingers into wooden bowls filled with mashed bitter fruit. Odder still, they wrapped large leaves around a thin red pea pod to munch between waving the thing in the air as they talked.

And talk they did. The Leader and his Right Hand relived the short game over and over, ascribing luck to this move, skill to that. Drail and his Hand of Victory often spent time analyzing a game for mistakes and areas to improve, but even they never debated the thing for an entire meal. Now mere spectators argued over the likelihood Manten could make the long shot again, or had he missed, the chance Bran's team would have won.

Surely a pointless conversation.

Bran himself, who seemed partial to the pea pods, had other words on his tongue. "Your team is skilled. Surely too skilled to leave the Great Continent for us."

The conversation around them paused. All waited to hear the answer.

"We wished to try our might against a Terrin team," Drail replied in his easy way.

Tryst caught Jason's look of approval, and had to suppress his grin. Jason thought Drail used clever subterfuge, but the gamesman merely spoke from his heart.

"Seems a long chance venture for a short chance gain," the Right Hand rumbled. Terrin voices were gravelly, as if strained through a very rough throat.

Jason licked his fingers, head tilting down as if looking at his plate. "Do Terrin ever travel to the Great Continent to play?"

Tryst knew that ploy. His defense master was carefully watching the Terrin through his eyelashes.

"Long chance venture for no gain at all," the Leader said. "Terrin do not leave our home."

Reading expressions on fanged faces proved impossible. Yet most likely - or the shortest chance, as his host might say - was these particular Terrin had not left the Dim Continent.

"Surely Terrin have traveled in the past," Tryst said. "Some of you must have seen the Great Continent."

The Leader peered at him for several blinks of the sun. Then, "You skins value the attraction of your homeland too high."

Jason sent him a swift glance at the Leader's delay.

Customs vary, of course. None knew that better than Tryst. On the surface, however, the Leader's reply had taken too long.

He guessed the Leader and his people had never left the Dim Continent, and had no desire to do so. But the Terrin knew something, if only rumors.

Of that he was sure.

On the journey to the first Tower, Marra often traveled between the two elders. Now she deliberately followed in their wake.

Kirth seethed, her lips pressed thin against the anger threatening to spill out. Marra had never seen the elder lose her temper before, and could only wonder at her reaction. Tinge, too, was silent, and though that was not unusual, the Terrin did seem profoundly annoyed.

The sun grew warm in the afternoon, and as the trail lead out in the open there was no cooling shade. Moist patches spread between Marra's shoulder blades and beneath her arms. Either the temperature was worse than that of the desert, or her time in Missea had lessened her resistance to it. She watched Kirth carefully for signs of heat exhaustion, though viewing the elder's back made that challenging.

At last a stream appeared, surrounded by trees clustering close to the rushing water. Tinge perched upon a fallen log, drinking long and deep from an odd-shaped water pouch. Marra hesitated, as Kirth merely leaned against a tree while she drank.

The Terrin gestured to the log before speaking. "Sit, my friend. This is the last pleasant stop we will have for days."

Marra gratefully dropped to the grass before realizing Kirth remained on her feet.

"You brought me to that Tower many years ago," the elder stowed her water. "Did you know then it was a sham?"

The Terrin's fangs grew long, but Marra doubted it was a smile. "I did."

"I always thought Agben had a law against lies," Kirth said. "That we agreed, Terrin and Skin, to faithfully share knowledge. That being of Agben was a stronger bond than any difference of species."

"We have not broken faith. I have not broken faith." Tinge plucked out a grain ball, but took no bite. "The Tower of Zaria stands deep inland. Unlike Agben, the priests had no desire to mix with skins. For centuries they sent only parts of the prophecy, bits of teachings. It was never Agben's place to question Zaria.

"Then, when I first became a student, Zaria changed. They set the small tower on the coast, inviting skin priests to come and share. When you asked to visit the Tower, I took you."

"I was told that was *the* Tower. The Black Tower on the Dim Continent."

"You told yourself that. And we - the Agben Terrin - were not free to share the truth."

Kirth stayed standing for a blink of the sun. And then, finally, she sat. "Why do you share now?"

"Because of Zaria's deception. They lie to you skins - they lie to me. Whether the lie is told to Agben Terrin, or to female Terrin, they lie."

"Lie to female Terrin?" Marra gasped, and wished she'd held her tongue.

Kirth looked at her for the first time that afternoon. "Remember the Terrin sexes live separately."

Tinge nodded at Marra. "One may have secrets. There are many things not told to Zaria, things not shared with the men of my land. But a lie is blasphemy...it goes against the goddess Eutykia." And at Marra's confusion, she added, "The goddess of luck. The seventh constellation to the north."

"Did you escort Rain to the second tower?" Kirth asked.

The Terrin shook her head. "When she asked, I took her where I took you. But on her next visit, she insisted on going alone. She repeated that every visit after, staying longer each time."

"Or traveled to the true Tower?"

Tinge shoved the last of the grain ball between her fangs, and licked her fingers. "I would never have believed it before today. But now - yes. Yes, I think it quite possible someone took her to the true Zaria Tower."

Marra watched their faces. Kirth furious, anxious. Reading Tinge's feelings beneath her fur was more challenging, yet her fangs had almost disappeared, which must mean something. Her voice sounded...rattled.

Or Marra might just be imagining her own emotion in the Terrin.

As the days passed, Marra found herself anxiously watching Kirth. The elder's mood did soften, if exhaustion could be labeled softening.

Tinge set a hard pace. They hurried over soft grass, hacked their way through heavy foliage. At one point, in a sleep-sling suspended from a single leaf with a stalk thicker than any desert tree, sudden rain poured down so hard she couldn't even see the other slings when she chanced a peek. Tinge pronounced it a day of rest. Pondering the lack of anything to do, Marra fell asleep.

She woke to the sun poised at the same point on the horizon, and gradually realized a whole day had passed. The steady drum of rain was gone, replaced by an odd symphony. Birds, she realized. Whole flocks of them.

Carefully splitting the folds of her sling, Marra levered out to step on vine-covered rocks. Kirth's snores gently trembled one of the two sleep-slings. The other dangled empty in the breeze.

Soft rustling noises drew Marra around a tall and hugely wide bush - or perhaps it was a short tree. She found Tinge squatting on the ground, fingers busily weaving long grass threads.

"May I help...?" Marra's voice trailed off as she realized she had no idea what the Terrin was doing.

"No, little Marra." The fangs lengthened in amusement. "Does Kirth still sleep?"

Marra nodded.

"Tis good to let her wake naturally today. Eutykia was kind with her storm - I forget how quickly you age."

"But...we all age each year."

Tinge purred deeply, laughing. The first laughter

she'd heard in days.

"All things age. Leaves dry to brittle flakes, falling from branches to crumble in the grass, yet their trees may still be standing centuries from now."

Digesting this, Marra studied the Agben elder. "And Terrin?"

Another purr. "You are not slow, skin girl. I am two hundred and forty years old."

Marra gaped.

"My species lives to three hundred and beyond. Steen the Wise, our most revered Agben elder, is said to be three hundred and thirty."

"You must learn so much!"

"Apparently we do not."

If it had been Kirth speaking such, Marra would have probed her meaning. With the Terrin, however, she felt too uncertain.

Instead she focused on the odd pocket Tinge was weaving. "What is that?"

"Reeder net," Tinge said, and set her hand on the ground to push her legs straight. She'd seemed so comfortable squatting, as if it were a natural position for her, and now struggled awkwardly to stand. Not sure if she should assist, Marra kept still.

The Terrin adjusted her hips before standing tall, and then brought her hand out to display the grass weaving spread between her fingers. A sort of webbing pocket looped through the Terrin digits, opening and closing with a gesture of her fist.

"Reeder net?" Marra asked.

"I got the idea from fishermen."

Tinge strode toward the thicker part of the jungle. Marra followed.

The plants merged here, grasses and shrubs and trees so close that branches tangled and leaves thrust each other aside. She couldn't judge where one plant ceased and another began.

Tinge snatched up two fallen twigs and handed one to her. Marra said nothing, yet the Terrin seemed adept at reading her expression.

"Do as I do and keep it before your face," the elder explained. Holding the stick half an arm's length out before her, she moved into the denser jungle.

Marra followed.

Tinge walked a few steps, her large furry head swiveling side to side, peering into the green leaf shadow. She stopped suddenly.

Slowly raising her hand with the Reeder net, she swept through the delicate foliage, murmuring low in her throat. Then, tugging a glass vial off the Terrin sash, the elder shook her gathered prize over the rim, and sealed it inside.

Curious, Marra stepped close enough to see the shiny green specs moving within.

"Reeders," Tinge told her. And led the way back to the sleep-slings.

Following, Marra pondered the Terrin's actions. "The first discipline is to heal," she mused. "The second is to enhance. The third...does it somehow..."

"Influence," Tinge rumbled.

"Influence. You influence living things by using bits of themselves!"

"Or affect other creatures with their properties."

King Bactor, Marra realized. Rain must have used some essence, hair or nails or something, to make them all believe a Terrin was the Skullan king.

"Not influence," Kirth snorted. "Pervert."

The elder Skullan sat on a log in their camp clearing, chewing a grain ball. "If you won't accept ignorance, little Marra, then learn the whole truth. To heal is to restore natural balance. Permanently, if done well. To enhance is to gently guide the body to a new pathway. With wise application and patience, it might also be permanent.

"The third discipline seeks to fool the body. It is a lie, and by its very nature cannot be good."

Clearly annoyed, Kirth's glare singed Marra's feelings. But now that the subject was broached, she needed to understand. "The bug repellent - was that not useful? To keep the insects away from Tinge's home while allowing the sun and breeze inside?"

"At the cost of killing the insects."

"But Rain did not kill Tryst." As soon as she spoke, Marra bit her lip. How much did Kirth want Tinge to know?

Tinge was gazing at Kirth, who flipped her hand in an impatient gesture. Giving permission - not to

Marra, but to the Terrin.

"One can create influencers," the Terrin rumbled, "With bits of creatures instead of whole creatures. But the more powerful the desired outcome, the more essence must be provided. I know not how Rain did what she did, but a heavy sleeping draught for skins could well be done without parts of that particular skin."

"By using creatures that sleep a lot?" Marra frowned.

"By using other skins," Kirth replied. "And judging by how well it worked, someone - some skin - most probably died."

The next village was three days march. Drail relished every step.

He'd prodded Adeena to ask the Right Hand for the best place to take them. He wanted a real game, not just one easy mark. And he wanted to watch Terrin play.

Drail wouldn't admit, even to himself, the other idea bubbling in his head.

It was only after they started the journey that he discovered Jason had intended a different tack. "Our mission," the Defense Master told him quietly, trailing far back from the guide's lead, "is not to dominate the Terrin comet arena."

Arguments rose to his lips - about the importance of maintaining the appearance, of keeping doubt from Adeena's thoughts. Instead Drail clamped his mouth shut.

Jason gave him a hard look. "In the future, let me ask the questions."

Their next comet game played against the standard three opponent teams on the field. The competition was better, but not overly so. The Hand of Victory easily claimed its second win.

In the feast that followed - it seemed such feasts were part of the comet day experience - Adeena took charge before Jason spoke, asking for the best village to mount their next challenge. And from the man's scowl, Drail knew he would be blamed.

So he sought to assuage his own curiosity. "Do Terrin play comet?"

"We love the game," the Leader's Right Hand growled. "Eutykia herself takes a hand. The greatest glory awaits those who compete in the Gathering Game."

"The Gathering Game?"

"Every five years the villages gather to share old stories and new ideas," Adeena explained. "Most Terrin attend. It's a rare village that does not send a leader or Right Hand."

"Have you been?" Jason asked her.

Lowering the pea pod she munched, Adeena shook her head. "The Gathering occurs once every five years. And before you ask, gamesmen, the next Gathering is three years away. I cannot escort you through the jungle for quite that long."

No rumble-laughs greeted her sally, which was unusual. Male Terrin always indulged the girl guide.

Instead the Right Hand spoke. "The Gathering is three moons away, little Adeena. We ourselves leave in a handful of days."

"But..." the girl's voice died.

"Would skins be allowed to attend?" Tryst spoke quietly.

The Right Hand turned to his Leader. The two shared a long, long look.

"You will be our shaka. Our gift to the Gathering," the Leader said.

They wasted two more days before setting out from the village. Tryst begrudged every blink of the sun.

A Gathering occurring between Gatherings did not bode well. Jason counseled that such activity meant further attacks, deeper plots. That they were being sent to it suggested not all Terrin were in on the plot - which made sense. The whole Skullan race was not told of the King's more dangerous plans.

Their expensive guide needed directions, which apparently proved complex. Adeena spent an entire midday meal alone with the Right Hand, only to meet again with the Leader for the whole of the afternoon. Why they could not travel with the village was never fully explained.

As preparations for the evening feast began, Tryst fumed.

Drail slapped his shoulder encouragingly. "She's careful, which is as it should be. This is not a place to wander lost."

"Each blink of the sun favors the Terrin. More time to plan, more time to act, and less time for our response. All due to a girl's confusion."

"That's unfair," Drail told him. "Skins have never traveled to a Gathering. The terrain may be vastly different, the path unmarked. We should trust her."

"You seem to trust her enough for all of us."

"She's clever. And has courage."

"Unlike Marra?" Tryst demanded before he could stop himself.

Drail gave him an odd look. "Marra is very brave." He spoke as if explaining something to a child. "Adeena has confidence, so she carries her courage on her shoulders. Marra's confidence is a mere seedling. Her courage is the willingness to proceed regardless."

As the gamesman strode away, Tryst acknowledged the truth of his words. Adeena strode proudly through the world, while Marra slipped quietly on her way. Yet the desert girl faced every challenge head on, never wavering. He'd come to admire her unfailing determination to do the right thing no matter the consequences.

Adeena reminded him of the noble ladies his grandsire wanted him to marry. Secure, demanding...tall. And he had no use for any of them. The only warmth he felt for any female was for a

Trumen nobody who had saved him on the Flats of Beard.

Tryst turned on his heel, looking for Jason. He needed to occupy his mind with strategies for the Gathering.

If delay tried Tryst's patience, the actual journey tore it to shreds.

The jungle steamed in the heat, coating the skin in slick sweat. Beneath the foliage, briers snatched at legs and clothing. The boots Adeena had insisted they needed proved her correct.

A handful of days in, the heavy vegetation gave way to a dusty wall of rock. The trees pulled back, the path wound round what appeared to be a gigantic spherical boulder. Circling it, Tryst felt dwarfed by the vast shadow.

Beyond that stretched a steep rocky cliff, which Adeena promised held an easy path, or so she'd been told. Either they never found it, or Terrin possessed climbing skills not physically apparent.

The only consolation was their guide fared worse than their party.

The base of the cliff required careful path selection, but near the summit - high enough that Tryst refrained from looking over his shoulder - the terrain demanded advanced climbing skills. Fortunately Jason had taught him how to wedge a hand into a gap and use his toes to advantage.

The only reason he didn't like looking down was it reminded him of the last climb he'd attempted, hoping to reach safety in a cave. On that day he'd failed.

The desert men scampered up effortlessly, joking as they swung from hold to hold. Desert children, it turned out, often played on rocky hills because it developed muscles for comet. And perhaps, he suspected, there was little else to do on the Flats of Beard.

Which left Adeena as the only one unable to climb the last third of the cliff.

Drail coached, encouraged, and finally carried her to the peak. Several cutting remarks rose to Tryst's tongue, and only the sight of the girl's quaking limbs kept him quiet. When she tried to continue, the gamesman insisted they rest, and unearthed his own waterskin to quench her thirst.

As she sat among the shale, torn between embarrassment at her own frailty and gratitude to the Leader of the Hand of Victory for shoring her up, Tryst suddenly understood his reactions.

Irritation at the girl for not being Marra - and a cold fury at Drail for betraying her.

For the three weeks they traveled, Drail enjoyed the journey.

It was a wild land filled with varied life, both plant and animal. The terrain morphed from soft and thickly green - outdoing the Great Continent - to red and granite hard, as if imported from the Wavering Continent. Adeena even described bitter cold in the northern mountains, where frost piled on frost. The only thing missing was comet, and since the local skins offered little competition, and playing Terrin seemed both unlikely and unhealthy, for the moment he was content to travel.

The others were not, he knew. The Skullan of the party chomped at the bit like horses anxious to gallop headlong across the land. His teammates disliked the strange continent, wanting to finish and go home. Even Adeena acted skittish, no longer sure of her path on several levels.

At the end of the third week they reached a sort of string forest.

The trees stood shorter here, with dangling threads for leaves as soft as the down on a newly hatched duckling. The slightest breeze stirred rippling waves all about them, like a deep green sea. Drail would have doubted any man describing this place if he hadn't seen it for himself.

Many strings brushed across his face as they walked, startling and a little unpleasant as he felt many more than he saw. Drail assumed the leaves were so tiny as to be invisible.

Instead they turned out to be webs spun by tiny green insects.

Adeena was the first to discover this. "Yute save me," she cried, brushing at her hair to dislodge anything that might cling there. She wound a gauze cloth around her head to protect her face as best she could manage.

The others followed suit with bits of cloth cut from a spare sleep-sling. Harmless the creatures might be, but finding your face suddenly encased in an invisible web was most disconcerting.

When at last they emerged from the trees, Adeena tore the gauze from her face and flung it away, frantically brushing at her hair in case any stray bug lingered.

Laughing, Drail stepped to help her, plucking a few lingering threads from her blond tresses. Adeena stared up at him, a mingled look of sheepishness and defiance.

Impulsively he kissed her.

Relieved to be clear of the string-threaded forest, Tryst freed his face from its covering just as Drail kissed the girl. His temper, which had been sorely tried recently, leapt into his throat, demanding to shout.

Adeena stepped back, though the soft look in her eyes suggested she liked Drail's gesture. Likely she would have called a rest period if Jason had allowed it. Instead the Defense Master pushed them on.

Clamping down on his anger, Tryst drew up beside Drail as they journeyed on. "What about Marra?"

Many men would have shown confusion,

pretending they had no idea why the question was posed. Drail was not of their number. His brow lifted - not at the audacity of the question, but in consideration of the genuine answer. "Marra and I are both desert born. We'll likely end up together on the Flats, raising fine sons. Sons who will play in games greater than any yet played."

Yet as he spoke, Drail's eyes followed Adeena.

"When your comet days are done?"

Drail nodded.

More questions welled up - about exactly when that would be, or what Drail would do in the meantime. And did Marra truly want to leave Missea and Agben? Tryst refrained from asking them, but only just.

Because to his own ears, he sounded less a concerned friend than a village snoop.

With the sun setting at his back, Drail made himself comfortable before the small fire. It was stoked for heating water rather than people, yet the flames provided a cheery spot to gather. They hadn't allowed themselves tea in days, and sipping it now was a treat.

"How much farther to the Gathering?" Jason asked.

"I do not know," Adeena replied. "We travel another day, perhaps two, to the village by the goss trees. The Leader there will take us to the Gathering."

"Goss trees?" Drail asked.

"Another village?" Tryst demanded.

The girl waved at the string forest behind them and

turned to face Tryst. "We are in an area I have never seen. And it would not be...prudent...to burst upon the Gathering without Terrin escort."

Clearly the Prince was not happy, though Drail found her explanation reasonable. If this Gathering held the importance the Defense Master thought, surely a party of Skins would not be warmly welcomed.

"But this Leader will escort us?"

"If we declare ourselves shaka. So I was told." Doubt clouded her eyes, and the conversation ceased, though clearly the Skullan had much to say. Drail expected questioning to resume at any time, but no one spoke again.

With no trees near, sleep-slings were spread across the ground. They slept as best they could.

5.

KIRTH WAS ALREADY regretting this
journey.

The land they faced the next day sloped
ever up, moving them higher and tiring Kirth quickly.
As the jungle did not thin, the path itself grew more
troublesome, and the ache in her back demanded
more rest periods.

Rain had been her responsibility, even if the woman
had studied under anyone who would teach her. Kirth
should have recognized her ambition, her blindness to
the bars of decency. Agben still debated crossing that
line between healing and enhancing; it never occurred
to her that Rain would eagerly pursue the third
discipline.

On the path ahead, she watched Marra's careful

steps, trying to avoid the thorny foliage despite wearing the odd jungle pants. Marra was a good girl, she knew. Yet the young apprentice also had a thirst for knowledge - and now an avenue to satisfy it.

Still, Marra was very different. Rain had sought power, prestige. Rain would keep secret all she learned, to make herself more powerful. Kirth had watched Marra show others how to use a tube to extract, or judge a brewed potion to be properly heated.

Marra had that humbleness Trumen so often displayed. She shied away from power and attention. And deceit was foreign to her.

"Stop." Tinge held a paw out behind her as she scanned the thickening jungle. "We need goss sticks."

Kirth frowned as Marra plucked two sticks from the ground, brushing the dirt away before handing one to her. She'd never heard of goss sticks; so how did Marra know?

The little Trumen must have read her thoughts. "Tinge used one earlier."

Behind the girl, Tinge quivered with amusement. "My friend, we are close to our destination. Let us get through this last bit, and we can make tea and talk."

The Terrin turned, leading them on through thickening jungle. Marra peered up at Kirth - with concern, she realized. Stars, if she doubted the little herb girl, she might as well just give up.

At times the plants receded slightly, allowing the sun to trickle through. Its beams highlighted intricate webs, allowing Marra to avoid them. More often the thick branches obscured the light, rendering the strands invisible. Twice her stick dipped too low, and the resulting web engulfing her face were repulsive. Her fingers brushed hastily to clear it from skin and hair.

The goss stick, held at a proper distance, swept the path clear. Well, the path before her face at least. Marra hated to think of the web accumulating on her clothing, along with any of the tiny Reeders. A bath and a thorough scrub would be most welcome after this, she decided. No matter how cold the stream.

The goss jungle never thinned - it simply stopped altogether. Squeezing between two trees growing very close together, wincing as branches snagged her hair and clothes, Marra popped through into the clear.

Suddenly a carpet of delicate moss stretched before them, peppered with clumps of wildflowers painted aqua and violet and scarlet. And then she noticed the Terrin.

Some distance ahead, far enough she couldn't see individual faces, a cluster of them sat on the moss. And beyond them a second cluster, and a third beyond that. Still more, she saw, to the south. It wasn't until she heard Kirth's gasp that Marra looked north and saw the Black Tower.

The Tower of Zaria.

At the apex of the hill it stood, above a stone wall on a ragged ridge at odds with the gentle green field. The Tower soared into the air, so black it appeared more a hole in the sky than a structure made by man. Surely of the same poured stone used in Missea's black arena, only more ominous. And tall enough that mists shrouded the upper half.

Not mist - smoke. Seeping out of holes oddly spaced on the facade. Old tales tickled Marra's memory, of fire dragons whose nostrils poured such smoke.

"I thought Terrin disdained such fancy structures as we skins like to build," Kirth glared at Tinge. "I thought living within nature, within the land was the way of your people."

"It is," Tinge told her gently. "This thing dates back before memory. The Zaria priests claimed it to house the scrolls."

"There must be a lot of scrolls," Kirth said dryly.

Marra had always been a little nervous of the Black Arena. What she felt now, approaching this Black Tower, bordered on terror.

It looked unnatural, so deeply black against a brilliant blue sky. Chills stirred the hair on her arms despite the midday's warmth, as if the very structure sucked the heat from the air.

They passed near - but not too near - a cluster of Terrin heating pots over low-banked fires. Perhaps it was nearing time for the evening meal, Marra thought. If so, her stomach was unusually silent. The Terrin worked at the same plodding pace as Tinge, seemingly ignoring them.

Although more than a few heads turned as they passed.

Tinge marched up the steps cut into the stacked stone wall, striding straight to the black cylinder. Squinting, Marra couldn't see any sign of a door. The Terrin rapped on the slick wall, the sound oddly similar to that when a glass vial struck a stone table.

She saw nothing - even when a crystal tinny noise vibrated through her. The door was half-swung open before she knew it had yielded, and then it yawned before her, an opening wide enough the three of them could pass through abreast. The door itself Marra could only judge by the shape of the opening, for the black portal against the Black Tower was impossible to see. Reluctant to leave the sunshine, she entered only because she was more reluctant to part from Kirth and Tinge.

The interior was just as black, with the same shiny surfaces of the arena. These, however, were lit by braziers evenly spaced on the walls, revealing cushioned couches, soft rugs, and elegant tables with glass pitchers and matching goblets. A room in its way as luxurious as any she'd seen in Tryst's palace.

A fluttering near Tinge drew her attention to a Terrin so large he loomed over the female of his species. He wore a white robe - which meant he was an acolyte.

"What chance led you here?" he growled.

"The wisdom of Agben," she growled back.

His body swelled, his eyes flashed. Marra honestly expected him to strike the female where she stood - and then the Desert Crane save them all.

Tinge, however, turned her back to him, striding to the most prominent chair, lowering herself with a regal authority worthy of King Bactor. She motioned for them to follow her example.

"I am not here for pleasantries," she rasped, waving her hand dismissively. "Go tell your High Priest I demand to see him."

His glare was a threat to Tinge, to Kirth. For an instant Marra thought he intended to smite them all.

And then he shut the outside door and vanished.

Tinge waited till the acolyte left to do her bidding.

Then she reached to pour herself a goblet of water, satisfied to see no trembling in her hands. For she was angry.

Very angry.

Male Terrin treated females with great respect. All Terrin treated Agben - skin or Terrin - with great respect. It was the way of things. So to encounter such hostility, such insolence in a second year acolyte infuriated her as she hadn't been in a century.

"He seemed...reluctant," Kirth probed.

Tinge poured two more goblets of cool water. "Zaria seems to have altered recently."

"How recently?"

It was a good question. Rubbing her itching neck, she sighed. "I've not been to this tower since before Rain first stood on the Dim Continent."

"Rain has diverted the proper course of things," Kirth said. "Yet I find it difficult to believe she could affect Terrin so easily."

Tinge agreed. "No Zaria priest - no Terrin male - would allow..."

She broke off as a small priest, as proclaimed by his red robes, appeared. He bowed, gesturing. "Lady, if you would please to follow me."

Marra and Kirth rose with her; she felt the priest's startled reaction and forestalled his words. "Wait here, my friend."

Kirth nodded. She and Marra sat again, seemingly comfortable to wait as long as required. But the elder gave her a swift look, bespeaking her concern.

It was a look, Tinge realized, that the priest would not grasp. Perhaps she had spent too much time with the Agben skins as of late.

For by Yute, she hadn't spent enough with Zaria Terrin.

Marra lifted her goblet, but couldn't drink.

Her surroundings were so odd. Furniture as cozy as it was pretty, matching the blueish rug that kept their feet off the cold stone floor. But with no windows and no sunlight, she felt imprisoned in a small pocket of comfort surrounded by evil shadows. A pretense of safety as much an illusion as the Terrin impersonating King Bactor.

"Kirth...." she began, but the elder silenced her with a gesture.

The Terrin acolyte returned. "Come."

He led them down the same hall Tinge had taken. In the dim light his white robes were rapidly consumed by shadows, making it necessary to keep her eyes on him. Marra could just make out hollows in the walls, evenly spaced black voids where doorways probably stood. Whether the black indicated shut doors or open rooms not in use she could only guess.

The passage veered right. A black void appeared on the left, this one flanked by torches burning on either side. Lifting one from its holder, he stepped inside.

Marra could barely discern stairs leading up. The acolyte passed these, choosing a second stairway descending into the dark.

By the Desert Crane! It seemed the many levels above were not enough - there were levels below. How many floors did this Tower contain?

With the shiny black surface of the walls, she lost any concept of how far they descended. The steps spiraled, and if there were doorways to levels they passed, Marra never saw them. Sounds of dripping water mingled with the rasping of his robe, and Kirth's gasping breath. The elder was growing tired.

"How much farther?" Marra asked, and winced at the loudness of her voice.

There was no reply.

Worried, she wanted to move beside her mistress, but the stairs were narrow and with only the wall itself for a railing. If they lost their balance, how far would they fall?

At last the stairs ceased. The acolyte veered down another hall, this one with no braziers, no light from any source save the flickering torch in the Terrin's grasp.

She felt rather than saw the doorway, and knew themselves in some sort of room. A stench of mold and worse warned her before the sharp click of the metal grid.

A grid separating them from the acolyte and his torch.

"We are of Agben," Kirth snapped.

"Welcome, Agben skins." And Marra glimpsed a last flutter of a white robe before the light retreated into the void.

Late afternoon they stumbled into the goss tree village. Stumble, Tryst decided, being the most accurate description.

Adeena appeared to be using all her wood-lore, eyes scouring the ground, fingers testing a broken branch.

It was the clattering of stones, however, that pointed them to their target. To his amusement the girl merely turned toward the noise, for all the world as if the broken branch had told her which way.

From a distance it appeared they headed toward a thick forest - before part of that forest suddenly swung open. A gate, opening within a disguised wall. These Terrin protected their village, either due to living close to the Gathering place or for some other reason.

Though the gate yawned wide, two Terrin blocked the path inside.

"What chance led you here?" growled one creature.

"A lucky path of intention," Adeena spoke firmly. "The Leader Qwin chose these men to be his shaka to the Gathering."

Qwin? This was the first Terrin name Tryst had heard, and he wondered if Adeena had known others she failed to mention.

"Qwin." Terrin expression were always difficult to read - but this did not look like welcome.

"Qwin proclaims I am to present these gamesmen of the Hand of Victory to his brother. Qwall is to share in this great shaka to the Gathering."

The guards turned to each other, fur quivering, fangs lengthening. They emitted a loud raspy purr.

Terrin laughter, Tryst realized.

Their entrance seemed in doubt.

Drail exchanged looks with Olver and Manten, both

seeming as little pleased as he was. None of the Terrin villages had welcomed them, but this one reeked of distrust. The guards blocked the entrance, waiting till other Terrin arrived and looked them over. Their discussion was low, rasping, and impossible to understand.

"Qwall will wish to meet us," Adeena insisted.

Despite a fierce frown, she drew her hands into her stomach - the girl's sign of tension. One of the lessons Raston had taught was observing opponents' outward signs of confidence, knowledge, and nervousness. Words could easily lie, but few knew enough to mask their signs.

And opponents who did that could not be taken lightly no matter their true feelings.

In the silence that followed Adeena's voice, he heard a distant scramble, thump. And then the cries of an appreciative audience, albeit guttural.

"Comet!" he said, and turned toward the sound. The noises came not from within, but to the far side of the wall. He strode off towards it.

And after the briefest hesitation, the others followed.

Rounding the wall, Drail saw the field surrounded by sitting Terrin. It was larger than usual, which was just as well, for the four teams of the massive creatures took a lot of space.

They looked huge out there.

The Terrin played on moss, as on the other fields

here. The only demarcation for the edge, as far as he could tell, was the sitting spectators. The cone in the center was the same hairy lump, the circle of darop teeth. What was different was the Terrin themselves.

The teams playing appeared to be the largest of their kind - fully half as large again as any he'd seen. On the Dim Continent they had always lumbered, moving with a clumsy gait. Now, thundering across the field, he remembered the speed that another Terrin in the Black Arena had shown.

Stars, they were fast for such large creatures.

"By the Great Goose..." Jason hissed.

The comet ball arced high through the air, to bounce off the cone. A Terrin caught it between his knees, and snatching it up ran toward the wickedly pointed teeth. At the last second he threw, successfully sinking it.

The crowd slapped the grass in approval.

Another ball dropped into the cone, and play was halted. Having sunk two balls, four of the Terrin - all with a wide red cloth tied around one arm - shuffled off the field to the steady beat of fists pounding earth.

When play resumed, the remaining comets sank quickly. A Terrin with a white cloth on his arm pulled the balls from the tail, and used his cloth to polish each, revealing the number of spots.

The red team won.

"I would not like to play these bastards," Old Merle murmured.

"I would," said Drail.

The sheer brutality of the game shook Tryst.

He'd thought the Terrin clumsy. Strong of course, but awkward in their odd bodies. He'd imagined them as poor warriors, neither equipped for a true battle nor anxious to fight. Already strategies to defeat them had brewed in his mind.

But the victorious gamesmen striding off the field belied that impression. These creatures relished the challenge, knew how to conquer opponents, perhaps conquer a continent.

The giant monster of the winning shot was striding towards them as a smaller Terrin told him, "The year has come for you to finally defeat the Bone Breaker."

Noticing Tryst, the champion gestured. One of the guards spoke up.

"Qwin says these skins are shaka."

Throwing back its head, fangs shooting toward the sky, the Terrin roared with laughter.

"My brother's jest!" it growled when able to speak. "He has outdone me again!"

Adeena stepped forward, sputtering indignantly. Undoubtedly she resented the joke at her expense. "We have traveled a difficult path for this...jest. Yute herself guided our steps...at the very least they deserve a sit down with Qwall!"

Tryst saw the change in atmosphere, the amusement vanishing at her speech. The large Terrin laugh-purred again, but his black eyes bored into hers.

"At least allow me to speak with your Leader," she demanded.

"As you will," the Terrin said. "What would you tell me?"

So the champion gamesman was also the Leader. History taught that such men were not rulers at all. They were conquerors.

The smaller Terrin beside Qwall spoke - not to them, but to his leader. "The game."

Qwall nodded, eyes on Adeena. "Approach the Gathering if you will. We shall not escort you."

Tryst saw from her face that was not an option.

The Terrin turned back towards the field.

"May we watch?" Drail called.

Qwall's head spun back, so far as to look grotesque. "If you wish," the Terrin rumbled. "See how the game is truly played."

Tryst saw Jason's reaction, his hand lifting to stop the desert man, hesitating. There seemed little to be gained by playing spectator. But truly, there was even less to gain by leaving.

So they strode across the hot plain.

The seated Terrin shuffled aside, leaving room and to spare. Though the gesture was likely meaningless, Drail smiled his thanks. No point in being rude.

Sitting among the creatures made him acutely aware of the size difference. Not just height, but sheer bulk. He must be insane.

Jason caught his eye and nodded approval. The Defense Master thought he'd done this to prolong the contact, maybe change their mind. He hadn't, of course.

Striding across the field, Qwall and his teammates loomed large. The sun behind them cast long shadows, making them seem like myths from some childhood tale. The smaller Terrin ran out, waving a red-colored waterskin. Qwall took it, squirting a shot down his throat - if throat it was - before passing it on. Drail noted the other teams performed the same ritual, each from a waterskin matching the color of their armband.

A Terrin version of Birr Elixir, he decided. Some potion to enhance their play.

The four teams took their place on the field. The large paws lifted, stabbing at the air before them, seeming to catch...something. An insect? Then they yanked back, closed fist to chest in a vaguely familiar gesture. Adeena's gesture, he realized.

Drail never took his eyes off the game.

The beasts' bulk slowed their movements, but less than he'd expect. Unlike Skullan, Terrin took wild shots at the comet tail early and often. He caught Old Merle's frown - his mentor had ripped men apart for such sloppy play. The occasional risk was worth it; too many rash throws doomed a team. That should give the Hand of Victory an advantage.

Which wouldn't be near enough to offset the Terrin mass and strength.

"You are mad," Old Merle murmured.

Drail nodded; he must be mad indeed.

Qwall ended the game with an insane shot, springing sideways as he hurled the ball without proper aim. The comet bounced off one of the tusks in the ring, deflected straight into the sky.

Players froze; spectators held their breath.

And then the sphere fell back to earth, hitting the rim, shooting skyward again. And dropping into the hole.

Whoops of glee punctuated the palm-slapping of the turf. Cries of "QWALL!" and "YUTE!" filled the air. Terrin or not, some things remained the same.

"That was pure luck," Drail said aloud.

"Yes," Adeena told him, her eyes shining. "He bathes in Yute's approval!"

The game finished fast, due to reckless throws and more reckless attempts to block. Drail wondered about their endurance - being so large they might lack it, even favor short games because of it.

It would be interesting to see how long Terrin lasted in a Skullan game.

Qwall stood ring center, fist raised to accept his due. Yute had smiled on him yet again.

Grinning at his people, he slowly turned until the skins rotated into view. Their eyes, so flattened against their naked faces, gawking in genuine awe.

That display had shocked the little band. They'd witnessed just how superior the Terrin race stood measured against their puny bodies. How mighty, how sharp. How favored by the gods.

Snatching the fivespot ball from the moss at his feet, Qwall strode toward them, wanting to demonstrate how little the hard-fought game had dented his stamina. Let them gawk and go home. Qwin's joke be damned.

Surprisingly, the skins rose to stand before him. Surely they were afraid. Surely they had to clamp down on the muscles in their funny legs to keep from fleeing in fear.

And even as he grinned at the amusing image, one of the skins held out its scrawny limb.

"Well played," it said. "May we challenge you next?"

Qwall's gaze jerked to the female guide. There had to be a different meaning here. These stupid skins couldn't actually want to challenge him. But the guide's wide eyes were directed not at him in hasty rebuttal, but at the one who spoke.

And in the resounding stillness - the world itself seemed to hush - it dawned on him that all his people had heard this challenge. By fall of night every villager would talk of the courage, the sheer audacity of these puny skins.

By Yute's own luck, he dare not refuse.

In the silence that followed, Drail caught the frozen reactions surrounding him. The open mouths on Olver and Manten and Adeena; Old Merle's shaking head. Startled respect from Jason, who still believed Drail's only concern was helping the Skullan mission.

"Daft fool..." Old Merle hissed.

The Terrin, every last one of them, stood stock still. Drail doubted they'd move if he suddenly hurled lightning bolts at their feet.

It was Tryst who broke the spell, stepping up to pluck the ball out of the Terrin's grip. The Prince tested its weight, its shape.

And grinned. "Shall we play just us - your team and ours?"

Drail found the Terrin very difficult to read. The creature ought to laugh in amusement, or snarl furiously, determined to crush their impudence. Even a mild calm would fit.

But the impression he got was a sort of cold...fear.

In twenty blinks of the sun Drail stood by the tusk-ringed cone.

Jason's glare seared him still. Jason had argued vehemently, wanting himself and not Tryst to play. Drail had argued back, insisting Tryst had the experience, not the Defense Master. Fortunately the Prince himself had simply strode onto the field.

The small Terrin with the white armband popped up, holding two waterskins. Something flashed in

Qwall's eyes, but he nodded before taking his swallow.

The second waterskin was offered to Drail.

He sniffed it, detecting a faint odor. If only Marra were here, she could tell him what it was. But even if their host's intent was good, how would the potion affect non-terrin?

He refused.

New balls, fully coated with comet dust, were set carefully around them. The Terrin selected one, Drail took another, and then picked a third at Qwall's gesture before the leader took the last. If nothing else, the creatures seemed scrupulously fair.

The Terrin trotted towards his team; Drail did the same.

Olver and Manten still looked stunned, though Tryst stood ready.

"It's just fun," Drail punched Manten's shoulder. "Nothing hinges on our victory. Just...play."

The judge barked something that might have been comet, and the Terrin all snatched at the air and struck their chests before moving - each looking as uncertain as his own men.

"They'll try to sink balls and end this fast. Block them!" Drail warned before racing to the center.

A blink of the sun later he heard the others running, feet muffled against the moss field.

"They'll kill us," Olver cried.

"Block the balls - not the Terrin," Tryst shouted.

The Prince had the right of it. For some reason the

Terrin shied from the physical aspects of the game, intending to shoot and be done. It would be interesting to see what they did when that failed.

He hoped.

Drail's feet pounded the turf, finding the odd grass added a tiny spring to his stride. Either the Terrin were slower, or hesitated to see what the skins would do, for he reached the cone well ahead of Qwall's shot and leapt to stop it.

The ball bounced off his fist.

Manten caught it on the run, racing away from both cone and Terrin. "Shoot!" Drail shouted as he sped across the moss, for he saw the creature suddenly spring to life, speeding toward him. Either to position for better shots - or to knock him out of his defending position. If the latter, he hoped he'd survive.

Facing the onslaught, Drail heard rather than saw a ball sink into the cone. The slish-sound, the spectator reaction. He didn't know which team had scored - and for the instant he didn't care as two hoary giants hurtled toward him.

Drail shifted his weight, balancing evenly on the balls of his feet. Ready. He watched their odd gait, the peculiar bobbing motion of their bodies. Nearing him, one reached out.

And swatted him like a bug.

Face-planting in moss, he just glimpsed the comet arcing overhead before hearing the hollow click as it struck a tusk.

Rolling, he watched the Terrin snag the ricochet, hold it aloft with one palm. And hurl it with that same swatting gesture.

The tell-tale slish followed.

For an instant time itself froze. If the first ball had also been the Terrin's, the game was over.

When Drail saw Tryst running, he knew it had not.

Manten slung the last ball. The Prince caught it, ducked an outstretched Terrin arm, and shot. At that distance, it would be a miraculous shot.

It wasn't - the ball arced too soon. The Terrin hovering over him relaxed, preparing to catch it. A fatal mistake as Drail sprang to his feet and jumped.

He meant to grab the nearby tusk to launch himself, belatedly recalling Adeena's warning not to touch it. So he grabbed the Terrin's hairy shoulder instead, vaulting up to Tryst's shot.

And directing it home.

The Terrin crowd erupted, pounding turf, gibbering excitedly. Whether thrilled or furious Drail couldn't guess. Qwall sprinted up, raised his arm and slammed the last ball into the cone. The two of them stood there, facing each other, panting hard.

It took forever for the judge to extract the balls, clear the dust. And lay them out.

The Hand of Victory had sunk the first ball, which proved to be the three spot, and the third ball, which was the no spot. Their total was seven points. Thus the Terrin had sunk the five and the one, and with two points for the second ball sunk, had won the day.

When the third ball was cleaned, and the winner clear, Qwall shot a fist into the sky. "YUTE FAVORS THE TERRIN!"

The villagers took up the cry, pounding the moss with their fists.

Drail and the others made their way back to the sideline.

"Excellent," Old Merle slapped his back. "But for luck you were victorious."

"Luck favors the Terrin," Adeena told him with a warm smile.

The celebration that night was crammed with food, drink, and dancing. An odd line formed of Terrin stamping feet and swinging arms. Other Terrin crouched low to pound the ground with the same rhythm. Soon the creatures stamped a path through the village, one giant leading the others on a random trek. Cries of "Yute favors Qwall!" and "Murgar beware!" occasionally rose above the revelry.

Qwall stayed in his honored place, drinking from a waterskin marked with squiggly lines. Probably Terrin ale.

"You played well," Qwall toasted the Hand of Victory with the drink.

"So did you," Drail grinned.

Qwall nodded, squeezing the last of the waterskin contents down his throat. Wiping his mouth, he slapped him on the back. "I will take you."

"Take me?" Drail asked. Beside him, Jason and Tryst froze.

"You are a worthy shaka, Skin Man. I will take you to the Gathering."

It was only two days travel.

Tryst honestly felt it was twice as long. He prodded the guide to ask the Terrin how much farther, but she seemed reluctant to do so.

His arm tired of holding a 'goss stick' before his face. The Terrin used sticks to clear the path of webbing, a welcome innovation. When he saw Adeena with a long, forked twig before her, he had to smother his grin.

That proved, however, the only amusement on the trek.

Qwall led them through the string jungle without a night's sleep, which Jason noted grimly. That hinted at a stamina far beyond their own. The Defense Master fell into conversation with Drail over this, and later confessed to Tryst that Drail had insight he'd not previously credited.

Because, Tryst knew, the Trumen's observations were made solely from a gamesman perspective. Drail's eye sought the strengths and weaknesses of a comet opponent; assessing a foe for the battlefield never occurred to him.

Perhaps the difference wasn't that great.

He himself watched the creatures, noting their

widely swinging gait as their large feet climbed over uneven terrain. Their arms tried to counter this by swaying the opposite direction, which proved challenging among the thick trees. Tryst guessed they weren't used to traveling thus.

But how to use that fact strategically alluded him.

The goss jungle, as Adeena now labeled it, grew thicker before suddenly vanishing altogether. One moment they pushed through a particularly tight mass of leaves, the next they stood at the edge of a vast clearing, dotted with Terrin camps as far as he could see.

What unnerved him, however, was not the sheer number of their enemy but the Black Tower dominating the top of the slope.

"Zaria," Jason murmured for his ears alone. "Working with Agben? And if so, who leads who?"

Rain stood gazing down at the Gathering field.

It was early, of course. Terrin would not fill the field for another moon, and surely they'd fill it to overflowing. No one would defy an edict from Zaria. Indeed, even as she watched, another band emerged from the goss jungle to set camp a short distance from it.

That was what bothered her. They all hung back on the fringes, far from the Black Tower. Like children sitting in the back of a boring herb class, ready to make good their escape. These Terrin ought to push to be up front, crowding the Tower's surrounding wall. Fight to be near the center of power.

But then, Rain didn't really understand Terrin. They were shy when they should stand proud; nervous when they ought to proclaim their superiority. Skeptical when they should accept wise counsel.

Bowag was far too skeptical.

Moving from the window - a horrid thing of black tint that dyed the sun to a rusty brown - she strode across the royal blue carpet. That it was royal blue she knew only from viewing it outside the Tower walls when it was first brought. Lying now on her chamber floor, hindered by the scant light from the brazier and the window, the color was so muted it could have easily been green.

She suppressed a memory of her beautiful Palace chamber, and left to seek Pinter.

Pinter knelt at the Pit.

Carefully he massaged the stones in his hands against his belly fir. His body fell into the Rhythm, swaying with the ebb and flow of Eutykia. The counsel he sought now was necessary to his soul; this must be done in accordance with all of the goddess's whims.

When he heard the door creak open, he froze.

"You are certain they will obey the Tower?" the skin-woman's voice demanded behind him. Always demanding, always devoid of awareness for whatever task he was performing. This one's eyes were so filled with the vision of herself that she rarely saw anything else.

"Never enter a Tower room unless instructed to do so."

"You no longer play a king, Pinter." Rain strode around him, fists on her hips, eyes glaring venom. "You are certain they will come?"

Pinter frowned. When he first played the skin monarch, she had accorded respect. Her awe had faded fast since their flight from Missea. "You have only to gaze upon the field to see them obeying the summons."

"Slowly, perhaps. Reluctantly. I see no enthusiasm."

Opening the sacred box, he gently replaced each stone into its soft hole. He would have to seek Yute's counsel later. "They are summoned at the wrong time - for a Gathering that should not occur for several seasons. Fear and doubt prevail, skin-woman, as well they should."

"You will address me as Lady!"

"And you have interrupted my ritual again, though warned against this. You plague me with the same questions, repeat the same doubts. I grow weary, Agben. If you insist on riding this high horse of yours, we may well discover which of us is truly more valued in Bowag's eyes."

Her glare rippled with fury; her hairless mouth thinned to a straight line. Bowag thought he held a little pet Agben eager to follow him, willing to obey the Tower. Bowag was wrong. This female saw herself superior to all, even males of her own race. This female expected obedience from Terrin as well as Skins - not because she had earned it, but because she thought it her due. And in her ignorance, she misinterpreted the deference Terrin gave to their females.

Females were rare; valuable. Difficult to woo. That made them special - not superior.

"Return to your chamber," he said aloud. "You will be summoned when it is time."

The lips thinned even more. For four full blinks of the sun she glared, before finally strutting off. She wanted to question his authority even when there was nothing for her to gain.

And though it was a truly sinful wish, especially for an Upper Priest of Zaria, he would enjoy watching her downfall.

Pinter was not surprised to find the Agben skin in the counsel room, admonishing Bowag, the High Priest. Bowag was bobbing his head in the way that seemed to satisfy her, though obviously paying no attention to her words.

Pinter bowed. "You sent for me, my Wisdom?"

"By Eutykia, I sought counsel again this morning, my Right Hand. It is possible now is the time to bring Agben into our vision."

Mid-tirade, Rain fell silent.

"All of Agben...or one devotee?"

Bowag's fangs lengthened in a smile. "The first step is one devotee. Her reaction will guide us to the next step."

"You have more to tell me?" the foolish skin demanded.

"Return to your room," Pinter growled. Her eyes flew from him to Bowag, seeking, studying. When she next spoke he had to acknowledge she was sharp when she applied her mind.

"Tinge?" she queried. "I should travel with you...I know her well."

Pinter shook his head, warning Bowag not to reveal anything. But the High Priest had no concerns for what this skin learned.

"Travel is not necessary."

"Tell me," Rain demanded. And winced at the sharpness of her voice. Fortunately, Terrin seemed incapable of detecting emotional nuances.

"I have told you that Skullan will prevail. Your kind shall wipe out the lowly Trumen."

Impatient, Rain nodded. This was obvious - any Skullan knew it.

"What I have not told you is the Agben Academy will come to serve the Tower."

Rain gaped. Bowag's face was impossible to read, but she guessed he actually believed that.

For years she had imagined herself the head of

Agben, creating a whole new position in the world that none had held before. The High Woman of Agben, akin to the leader of Zaria.

Now he hoped for her subservience? He was a bigger fool than she'd guessed.

"It is foretold. You cannot avoid it."

We will see, she promised herself.

"You, Rain, could be the first to swear fealty. You could lead your academy, show the way for the others." He actually stepped forward, extending his hand. Expecting her to fall to her knees and kiss his stupid ring.

Well, she had no problem casting promises to the Tower, though keeping them was an entirely different matter. But there needed to be a worthy trade.

"Tell me," she purred, "What other secrets lie in your scrolls?"

She had the satisfaction of seeing his hand drop.

In the pitch black that followed the acolyte's retreat, Marra heard Kirth slowly circling the cell, her tread underscored with a sort of hollow echo. "Mistress?!" Her own voice bounced back at her, overloud and forlorn.

She counted four drops of water falling in the distance before the elder's response.

"I'm right here. I suggest you seat yourself and get comfortable." Her calm voice was soothing, as far as that was possible.

"The floor must be filthy," Marra hugged herself, staring downward. To no avail - the darkness was absolute.

Kirth's steps paused, hesitated. And finally moved close. "Where are you, child?"

"Here." Marra held out a hand; the elder found it, holding it firmly as she lowered herself.

"What are you doing?"

"Getting comfortable," Kirth huffed.

"But how do we...."

"At the moment we can do nothing. I rely on Tinge."

The chill seeped through her skin, crept into her bones. Reluctant to touch even the floor in this awful place, only her own swaying convinced Marra to sit before she fell.

Her protective breeches insulated against the hard cold surface, but that wouldn't last. "How will Tinge find us?"

"She is of Agben, and a powerful Terrin female. She would not abandon us. Whatever assurances they want, Tinge will gain our freedom."

Even as Marra relaxed, another voice cut through the water drips.

"Indeed I would, my old friend," the Terrin's voice rasped. "If I were not a prisoner as well."

Marra surfaced slowly from her sleep.

Vaguely disturbed, disoriented, she blinked to no avail. Whether her eyes were wide open or closed, the black void remained. She sat up too quickly, propping a hand on cold glass. No, not glass - poured black stone.

So it wasn't a nightmare after all. They really were prisoners in a cell below the earth. Truth be told, the only thing that kept her from screaming her head off was Kirth and Tinge there to witness it. And, Marra told herself over and over, it could not possibly help.

This was the third day, if Tinge's belief that they were being fed both a morning and evening meal was correct. In truth she had no appetite, and the grain balls stolen from their own rations just made her stomach clench. But Kirth kept admonishing her to eat.

The two elders had debated their situation as calmly as if debating which vinegars produced the best tinctures for snow juice. Tinge, apparently in a cell just across the tiny hall, believed they would have to be released. Terrin males were somewhat in awe of their women, and adding in Tinge's standing as Agben, she doubted they would dare keep her long. Their arrival had startled the Tower, but as soon as the priests had some sort of plan, they would talk with her again. While Kirth had agreed this may be true, she pointed out that as their females lived alone without regular contact, Tinge herself could be missing for a long time before any alarm would be raised. And she and Marra would merit less consideration.

Yesterday, Marra had wondered wildly if she could

kick the door down. She had practiced self-defense with Tryst, learning body physics to increase power. She'd even jumped to her feet to find the grid, rattling it with all her frustrated might.

The idea proved foolish. At her best she was nowhere near as strong as the smallest Trumen man, and the grid was forged to secure male Terrin. Her head had sagged to bump against the metal in defeat.

"What are you doing?" Tinge's voice had cut through her frustration.

"Being stupid," Marra whispered.

"Ahh. A male solution won't work here, little skin-girl."

And Kirth, unbelievably, had laughed.

Now, as Marra rubbed an awful kink out of her neck, Kirth spoke with a decided undercurrent.

"Marra, prove me right. Tell me that you wear your herb sash round your waist."

"Mistress? Where else would I wear it?"

Tinge broke in impatiently. "But do you wear it now, herb-girl?"

Marra nodded, before remembering no one could see. "I do."

"Then by Yute's own luck, we have a chance."

The plan, it seemed, was to make a potion. "If we cannot employ a male solution, we shall try a female one. Rather, an Agben one," Tinge purred.

Water rations had been served in wide, shallow cups that could be used as bowls. With Tinge's own herb vials dangling on her sash, she proposed mixing Reeder Potion with her fingers. "What shall I use as a base?" she mused.

"Spittle," Kirth replied. "But how to administer?"

"Reeder potion?" Marra had never heard of it.

Silence, and then the elder beside her sighed. "Zaria Terrin use it."

"To aid teaching," Tinge said.

"To lull the student's resistance," Kirth corrected. "It helps them comply with instruction."

"Comply?" Marra remembered gathering the Reeders from the goss. "Reeders make them obey?"

Kirth snorted. "That's what we mean by influence. It perverts the will."

"I think these wills need influencing," Tinge rumbled. "Marra, did you collect any of the moss by my house?"

Catching herself nodding again, Marra swallowed to clear her throat. "I did, Mistress."

"What an excellent student you are."

The first challenge they faced was getting the moss across the gap between the cells. Tinge had observed the last feeding, noting the large doorways of the holds, the corridor between just wide enough for a Terrin to pass without prisoners reaching through the grids being able to touch him. Fortunately their cells were directly across, albeit slightly staggered. If Marra stood to the left side of the grid and lobbed her sash, it should reach Tinge.

Still, it was a nervous attempt. If she missed....

"Use the grid to orient yourself," Kirth warned. "Toss it straight across - not down the length of the hall."

Marra sagged at the metallic thud as the cloth struck home. Pouncing on the sound, Tinge easily located it, pulling it through the grid. "Which pocket, herb girl?"

Surprised, she had to think, imagining she'd just collected the moss. "Third one in from the right." Kirth had said something about Terrin's sense of smell, but Marra couldn't fathom it being so poor as to miss the clear distinctions of ingredients held near the nostrils. At least they looked like nostrils.

"And bray dust?"

"Farthest right."

Kirth laughed. "Excellent. But how...."

Sounds of movement, of the cloth sash opening, trickled through the dark. "Terrin," Tinge said as she worked, "are very sensitive on the center palm."

"Moss paste, bray dust, and Reeder," Marra gasped. "You're going to make them obey you."

"Attempt. The potion is a mild inhibitor; I'm strengthening it as much as I can with the bray dust."

"Does it have a cumulative effect?" Kirth prodded.

"It does. If they send the same acolyte, by Yute's own luck we may yet win free."

"Trevor seed," Marra whispered.

"Do you have Trevor seed?" Tinge ceased her motions.

Kirth laughed again. "She has Britta's Trevor seed. Will it add to, or detract from, the bray dust?"

"Add," came the answer across the void. "Most definitely it will add."

"First pocket," Marra said.

6.

TWO THINGS to remember about Terrin, Tryst discovered. They travel quickly, and they travel light.

When he embarked on his epourney long ago, each day of stately travel befitted a Prince. They woke hours after dawn, dining on elegant breakfasts prepared by chefs as the Royal guide described the day's schedule for his approval. The mid-day meal was leisurely, and oft times they stopped late afternoon to challenge each other in archery or swordplay. Servants erected large tents and cooking stations as they amused themselves.

Traveling in the desert, of course, had been an efficient process. Each man did for himself, and for others as he could. That had been hot, sweaty work with no room for playing the idle game.

The Terrin moved faster still. They carried very little - only grain balls and sleep-slings were deemed necessary. Not even weapons burdened their trek.

Did that mean they lacked weapons altogether? Or held no fear of enemies?

Camp had been rapidly settled. Small fires were laid, seemingly more for the light and comfort than any need of warmth. Although there were other types of warmth, he supposed.

The 'skins' - he was getting used to the label - shared a fire with Qwall and his comet team.

Tryst found his gaze returning to the Tower often. The silky black column dominated everything, even in the night. Strange fog seeped from it still, lit by odd, pale lights randomly set on the black cylinder.

"When do we play?" Drail broke the silence, leaning back against his pack. Looking relaxed, though Tryst knew he wasn't. The gamesman emanated that nervous energy - a touch of fear at facing the Terrin again, mixed with an eagerness to exorcise it in play. Tryst doubted Drail much cared what was at stake - if he thought of it at all.

"You may not challenge the Terrin," Qwall warned, and smiled at Drail's frown. "You will not need to do so."

As the night wore on, Qwall and the village Terrin came and went, mingling with the other Terrin clusters nearby. There was a comradeship Tryst hadn't expected - genuine friends meeting again after time and distance apart. Somehow the separate villages led him to think they would not like each other.

Exchanging a glance with Jason, he realized he'd been counting on that separation - believing they'd be less willing to join together for a common cause. A cause such as fighting skins.

So much for that theory.

At midday came the sound Drail waited for.

It had been a jovial morning, with sunshine and Terrin laughter flavoring the grain ball breakfast. Somehow the buzz of conversation dimmed beneath the growing noise of fists pounding turf to the roar of approval. When Qwall came to get him, Drail had already leapt to his feet.

Set in a ring marked by a stone circle near the Black Tower, four Terrin teams raced around the darop teeth. Dodging, weaving. Less contact than a skin game. And stars, they were big. Their gamesmen always seemed far larger than other Terrin - unbelievably so.

Then two players collided.

A crack rang out, surely the sound of bone snapping in two. A Terrin lay howling on the moss, his lower leg now bent in a near right angle. The creatures' limbs had always seemed slender to him, giving an agility unusual for the size. Perhaps fragility was the price.

In Drail's experience, a serious comet match would continue. Even casual games barely stopped long enough to remove the injured player.

This one halted abruptly.

Beside him, Qwall stilled. "We do not allow Agben to the Gathering," he told Drail. "All we can do is bind his leg and carry him to them."

"Will he be all right?"

"If the binding is properly done, and the healer is reached soon enough."

The fallen player was gently carried away. Drail sensed the hesitation that followed, the waiting.

"Bad, bad luck," Adeena murmured.

Finally, another Terrin shuffled into the circle to take his place. The game cautiously resumed. So cautiously, in truth, that he started when Qwall clapped his shoulder.

"Still thirst to play, skin man?"

Standing on the edge of the field, Drail studied the opponents.

They faced just one team, the winner of the previous game. Their uncertain demeanor defied his understanding until the Prince spoke softly. "They see us as more fragile than themselves."

He might be right, Drail realized. Perhaps Terrin felt awe at their courage to play after witnessing the broken bone. After all, if so grave an injury could happen to such big creatures - what might befall the skin men?

Stretching his legs, squatting low to feel the muscle ease gently, he caught Manten's eyes widening and followed his stare.

The last game had drawn spectators - but nothing like the hoard now squeezing in from all sides, lining the field three and four deep.

Adeena drew up beside him, brows set. "The skins who play on the Dim Continent do so with each other," she told him. "In my mother's generation many more came, some very good indeed. None ever challenged Terrin."

"We are honored," Drail answered.

"You are foolish," she shot back. "Why do you do this thing?"

It was the Prince, stretching his shoulders, who gave the reply she demanded. "What sort of shaka would we be to merely watch Terrin play?"

Smiling, Qwall held aloft his waterskin. "Drink this," he insisted. "You cannot show well for Yute without its power."

Show well. Qwall gave them no chance to win.

Drail snatched the offering and drank.

Standing beside Jason, Tryst waited.

The Terrin team had walked past, eying them up and down. Suspecting a trick, no doubt. Qwall and his cronies exchanged grins, eager to watch the game. Tryst could feel his defense master's disapproval, but at least the man held his tongue.

Until Qwall produced his red-marked waterskin. "You cannot show well without its power."

Nor with it, Tryst thought.

The Leader of the Hand of Victory drank and passed it on.

To his surprise, Tryst watched Manten, then Olver drink. Even if Drail had faked his swallow, he knew the others would not. They would not hesitate to follow his lead.

And knowing that, Drail would not have pretended.

The waterskin was placed in his hands. Raising it, he sniffed the brew, finding the aroma faintly familiar. Something of his royal training set in, for without hesitation he pretended to gulp.

Unlike Jason, Tryst suspected no foul play, no attempt at trickery. But sampling this potion held no advantage either. Just as winning this game held no advantage.

When they strode out to take their place, Manten suddenly smiled. "We can win this," he burst out, as if surprised by the thought.

"We can," Olver nodded.

The two marched with conviction, with confidence. "I feel bigger," Olver flexed his muscles.

"You look bigger." Manten swung his arms, loosening up.

Studying both men, Tryst detected no physical change. It would be interesting to see their play.

Watching his Prince take the field, seeing the man's feet properly set, evenly balanced, filled Jason with pride. If only King Ganny could see the son of his son now - the old man could naught be anything but impressed.

Though Jason himself felt fury at his own impotence.

He should be the one facing these monsters. Damn Drail to hell for...

"Do not let them do this," Adeena appeared beside him. Feeling his fingers curling into fists, Jason bit back a withering retort.

The smaller creature with the white cloth tied round its bulky arm placed the balls on the moss. The Terrin leader beckoned; Drail lifted one ball, and then another when gestured to do so.

A shout rang across the field; both leaders spun towards their team and flung the balls...no. Holding one back, the Terrin raced to the tusks circling the cone.

Drail chased it, moving a shade faster than the thing, which was something at least. But with those spindly knees flexing deeper than seemed natural the damned monster made wild cuts in direction that no Skullan could make. Facing them in battle would be difficult if their fighting skills were equally adept.

The Terrin launched the ball, missing his shot by a wide stretch of air. His teammate already stood in place to recover it.

Jason watched the Prince sprint up with his own ball, two Terrin hard on his heels. Tryst had never been tall, but seeing him now with the giant beasts closing in - his heart leapt into his throat.

One huge hairy hand shot out to swat the man - Tryst ducked, sprang up, and shot his ball.

Utter silence as it sank. Maybe, Jason admitted, Drail had a point. Tryst was better prepared.

"EUTYKIA!" the Terrin leader howled. And the frozen Terrin team sprang back to life.

Second ball in hand, Manten sped towards the center. Jason stared - for the blond gamesman looked bigger somehow, his head definitely above the ring of tusks. Surely that had to be just a weird angle...

No. Olver sprinted even closer, cutting off a Terrin aiming to block him, and damned if he, too wasn't larger. The man's muscled chest looked enormous.

Stars - had Olver always been that muscular?

Jason sought Drail, spotting him as he leapt to block a Terrin shot. Drail looked nearly as large as the Terrin spectators, just as tall, almost as wide.

By the Great Goose - the waterskin. The drink had made them larger, just as it must do for the Terrin. No wonder their gamesmen had always seemed huge.

One of the monsters cut Manten off, leaping before him, snatching the ball. When the creature's arm clipped the man he slammed to the ground and lay still.

Unlike the previous game, the Terrin played on.

Drail himself caught the ball when the Terrin took his shot. Spinning, the Trumen aimed and threw - but misjudged the hairy paw shooting out to deflect. The Terrin did *not* succeed - but Drail's shot missed.

Odd, that. Drail's accuracy was legend, even among Skullan.

The Prince, ball in hand, raced for the tusks. Two Terrin angled towards him at full speed, looming large against the backdrop of spectators, twice as tall, twice as powerful.

Tryst would not have drunk the potion - his training would prevent it. So now he lacked even that advantage.

Jason stepped toward the field - Old Merle held him back.

A second comet soared past the tusks and sank into the cone. By a Terrin hand, judging from the team reaction. A third ball followed rapidly, and the game ended.

Once again, the Terrin won the day.

It was the men returning, striding across the field side by side, that held Jason's attention. Tryst had always stood taller than the Trumen, though not by much. It was one of the reasons his Prince liked their company.

Except now, to squelch any doubt, the others were clearly larger, a full third larger. Tryst looked as diminutive as he would striding beside the largest

Skullan.

Jason decided to watch the Trumen carefully. If the drink showed no ill effects, the Prince must use it the next game.

That night, Drail shook his head over the celebration.

He sat at a small fire, watching the odd dancing as drunk Terrin followed each other in long lines, while others cheered them on. Sparkles fluttered around some of the creatures, like blue fireflies playing in their fur. When he saw Qwall with red fireflies, he understood.

Ashbark powder, Adeena called it. Apparently it glowed in the night.

The Terrin rejoiced as if they'd won Port Leet, instead of a minor game against very minor foe. Astonished that skins had dared to challenge them, and thrilled to have prevailed.

Confusing, that. Their bodies were so much more massive - had they ever doubted their victory?

Skullan never doubted they'd prevail over Trumen. Indeed, been insulted that the inferior race would dare to try.

Qwall's villagers celebrated as if they had personally launched the winning shot, downing gourds of mawk, their intoxicating drink. Far stronger than ale, he'd discovered, and refrained from taking more than a few sips. Though Olver and Manten had been less reluctant.

Across the flames stood Qwall, surrounded by red sparkles and waving his empty gourd. The Terrin grinned - at least, Drail thought the lengthening fangs meant a grin.

"You, skin," the leader rumbled. "You are true gambler!"

That, Drail had learned, was a high compliment on the Dim Continent.

"One would almost pit you against Murgar himself! He is the greatest of all the Dim Continent! He once crushed an entire team - left them littered on the field."

"I thought Terrin didn't play skins?" Drail prodded.

"It was a Terrin team!" Another Terrin appeared to snatch Qwall's gourd - this one also with red sparkles. It was Qwin, Qwall's brother.

"Qwin's mawk," he growled, slapping his sibling's shoulder.

"As good as Qwin's shaka!" Qwall turned. The two faced each other with lengthening fangs.

It took Drail a few blinks of the sun to decide they were happy to see each other.

"That joke," Qwin said, "seems to play on me."

"It would play better on Olipp," Qwall murmured. The two left.

Adeena appeared and sat beside him, her lips curving upward. "You are the talk of all the fires," she said.

"Why the reluctance?" Jason relaxed across the campfire. "Terrin hold all the advantage in mass and strength. Yet they seem almost fearful to play skins."

Across the flames Drail saw Tryst tilt his head, listening.

"The risk is all theirs." The guide wrinkled her nose, surprised they didn't understand. "If they win, it is only as expected. Terrin ought to win. But if Eutykia chooses to tease...the ill luck would spill onto the gamesmen. Perhaps even the village."

"All to lose and nothing to gain," Tryst murmured, with a meaningful look at Jason.

Drail snorted. In truth that attitude was beyond him. A challenge presents itself - one faces it. To do otherwise was to cower away in fear.

"Yute!" shouted a Terrin voice. And Qwall and Qwin returned, bearing a third Terrin between them. A third Terrin with red sparkles - another leader.

"See," Qwall rumbled. "He's small, scrawny. You cannot be so afraid to face him on the field."

The third Terrin looked Drail over with a slow, insulting perusal. This one lacked that hesitation he'd seen in the others.

"This is your champion?"

"It is," Qwin slapped the leader's back. "Do you dare, Olipp?"

"I'll play him now."

Before Drail could protest, Qwall stepped in. "Give the poor things time to rest," he murmured. "They tire so easily."

"Three days," Olipp growled. "When the Gathering is full, and all can witness our victory, we will play these scrawny skins."

Drail stood - the top of his head barely higher than the Terrin's stomach - and bowed his head in acceptance. With something suspiciously sounding like a snort, Olipp left.

It seemed the fear of losing was fast disappearing in a cloud of Terrin success.

The Obedience Paste, as they'd taken to calling it, was ready. Marra didn't dare think about what they'd do if it failed.

Normally the potion was boiled to release the Reeder influence properly. Tinge had settled for using more Reeder to base, along with the bray dust and three Trevor seeds. Kirth agreed, though Marra had once been warned never to use more than one.

At least Trevor seed did not need heat to work.

Marra worried about the consequence of breaking Agben rules. At the School they were taught not to test new mixtures on anyone who wasn't fully aware and agreeable to the risk. Kirth had declared this a reasonable exception, while Tinge snorted the word 'daft' under her breath.

Applying the goo to their jailer was the challenge.

In the end they rolled Kirth's water bowl across the gap to Tinge. Her own had been used to make the goo, and drinking from it now could have adverse effects. When they saw the first hint of light, heard footsteps approach, the Terrin quickly rubbed a thick coating on the bottom.

The torch warmed the area, gleaming off the metal grid before revealing the furry outline of Tinge. Marra clutched the cold metal barrier until Kirth tugged her skirt. She forced herself to retreat and sit on the shadowy cold stone.

The blazing torch itself appeared, held in a furry Terrin hand. But the speaker was not Terrin.

"Good evening," a familiar voice purred. And Marra's hope, so gently nurtured for hours, shriveled.

"Rain." Kirth spat the name, struggling to stand on her feet. Reaching to help, Marra was waved away.

Rain's long hair swayed as she pivoted, stepping close to the grid. "Did you seek me, Kirth? Follow me all the way to the Dim Continent?"

"I couldn't believe you would betray us."

"So you want to ask me if I have?"

Kirth and Rain locked eyes through the grid. Marra realized the Skullan hadn't seen her - and preferred to keep it that way.

"I wish to understand why."

Venom flared in Rain's face. "Agben was betrayed by you and your kind. Withholding knowledge, forbidding an entire discipline practiced by others. You are stuck in old ways, old woman."

"So you were bringing this knowledge back to share

with us? Argue, perhaps, before the Confer as to its importance?"

Rain flushed in the flickering light. "You would never have allowed that."

"Not after you kidnapped a king."

Marra thought Rain flinched. Did she honestly expect Kirth to be ignorant? Or had the harshness from her old mentor disturbed her?

"Little Marra," Rain noticed her huddled on the floor. "You've come a long way. I'm so glad to have you as our guest."

Hot anger welled, and Marra leapt to her feet. Furious words trembled on her tongue, but she bit them back. What use would they be?

"Impotent, Trumen girl? Isn't that your natural state?"

Kirth stepped closer to Rain, reclaiming her attention. "You're safe at the moment. So tell me why you did this."

"This," Rain glared, "is the alliance you yourself always wanted. A true partnership with the Zaria Tower." Something in Rain's voice suggested she didn't quite believe her own words. "The Tower moves now to fulfill prophecy. Agben joins with it, sharing the work."

"So now you are Agben," Kirth snorted. "Can you be so deluded you think to also share the reward? The power?"

The Terrin jailer appeared at her side, offering the

water pitcher. At Kirth's nudge, Marra brought the bowl to the grid so he could pour.

"I take my place in the future of our world," Rain sneered. Neither she nor the jailer made any mention of the missing second water bowl.

The jailer lifted the torch, ready to leave.

"Take this advice," Kirth said. "See those scrolls for yourself. Read the text - don't let Zaria interpret it for you."

The light was fast disappearing.

"Enjoy your stay, old woman," Rain's words echoed in the dark chamber.

In the silence after Rain had gone, Marra sank back to the floor. The darkness always seemed much worse after the crackling blaze of the torch.

"We can try it next time," she told herself as much as Kirth. "She won't come to gloat with every meal."

A rasping sound floated through the grid. Terrin laughter.

"Did it work?" Kirth asked.

"We will know soon."

"You tried the paste?" Marra gasped. "Even with Rain standing nearby?"

"The more that one uses her mouth," Tinge growled, "The less she heeds her eyes."

"But if it works...if she sees it work..."

Kirth sat beside her. "I have little faith in Rain's perceiving anything outside her ambitions - and not much more in the teachings of Zaria."

"So you also suspect the Tower's version of the scrolls," Tinge murmured. "Indeed, something is very wrong here."

"The race war," Marra frowned. "There will be a third. And the Trumen race may be wiped out."

"Early on there was a caveat," Kirth spoke slowly. "A warning that destroying one race would ultimately doom both. That portion of the prophecy has disappeared from Zaria's teaching - but I remember it from my youth. These days it seems the Tower encourages the war."

"I am far older than you," Tinge softly rumbled. "I remember a time when there had been no past wars."

"You lived through the two race wars?" Marra gasped. "The first was over a thousand years ago!"

"I mean," Tinge sighed, "That there never was a war. That just a few centuries back, the scrolls only warned to avoid a conflict. It's what I was taught, what I believed. And then one day an Agben skin told me there had already been two wars."

"Which skin?" Kirth demanded.

"You."

By the time the torch approached, Marra thought it was their supper.

Turning her head from the revealing flames, she wiped her cheek of tears. She didn't want the others to see what a coward she was.

Squaring her shoulders, forcing a calming breath into her lungs, it took a blink of the sun to realize the acolyte carried no food.

"Mistress," he hissed. "My abject apologies for being so late. The devil skin insisted on gathering herbs."

"Open the cell," Tinge growled.

Marra held her breath. Metal clangs echoed, the robes of the acolyte fluttered in the poor light. And Tinge's grid door stood open. She stepped out, pointing.

"That one as well."

Despite herself, a sob rose in Marra's throat when the grid before her swung clear. She willed her legs to cease trembling as she rose and turned to help Kirth.

"Lead us out of the Tower," Tinge commanded the acolyte. "We must not be seen."

"Yes, Mistress. The priests are at their supper now...that is why I waited to do your bidding."

Turning, the white-robed Terrin lead them to the stairs.

Marra realized she was holding her breath, straining to hear any warning sounds. Drawing a lungful of air released a sob trapped in her throat. Such utter darkness must have affected her deeply.

But she was free, she reminded herself. 'Twas foolish to let panic overwhelm her now - especially here.

Shaking herself, Marra willed her breathing to slow and deepen. In the stillness that followed, she caught the soft scrape as the acolyte shoved on a heavy door. It swung to reveal the brazier lighting of the first floor.

Where Kratchett stood watching them, still wearing his fox boots.

"Marra," he purred.

Though not in his nature, Kratchett had almost given up. Since setting foot on the Dim Continent, things had gone from bad to worse. Now, seeing the herb girl, it was reassuring how quickly his brain churned a plan.

"Seize him," the unrobed Terrin growled. The acolyte yanked his arm, forcing him up on his toes.

"Wait! Marra...do you know what they're doing? Their plans!"

The foolish girl only stared at him - but the old Skullan took in his words. "Do *you* know these plans?"

Kratchett nodded. "If the Prince will let me go, I will tell him everything."

"Prince?" Little Marra finally stirred.

Did she think him a fool? "I know he's camped outside. And I'm guessing the Terrin with him have no clue who he is." The stunned look on her face would have duped him if he'd not seen the man for himself.

"I can tell him everything," he hissed urgently. "The plans, the Tower layout. Valuable information for a very small price." They *had* to believe him.

The acolyte looked at the other Terrin, in much the

way Marra looked at the elder Skullan.

It was that Terrin - the Terrin *not* dressed in priest robes - that finally spoke. "I will see you are freed when this is all done. If, indeed, you have honored your promise."

It wasn't much of a guarantee. But it was the best he was going to get - and the priests might appear at any moment.

"Will you be with the Prince? I'll join you later."

He waited for the single nod of the furry head, and then spun on his heel and ran.

Their stealth through the Tower suggested their activities weren't common knowledge. If trouble did arise, 'twas only prudent he be somewhere else.

Fox Boots faded from Marra's sight and thoughts as the acolyte, white robe fluttering, continued rapidly on. She hurried after him.

When they first came into the Tower, the braziers had seemed so dim; now, after days in a cell devoid of light, the brightness of this muted glow actually hurt.

Sunlight would be brutal, she realized.

Tinge strode with the acolyte, seemingly unaffected. Kirth, however, stumbled into a wall, and might have fallen if Marra hadn't grabbed her. The elder's Skullan weight almost toppled them both.

Using a familiar couch to steady them, she guessed they were near the entrance. Was it the only way out? Wouldn't they be seen?

She heard the click of a latch and felt cooler air on her cheek, though she saw nothing. Forcing herself not to run, Marra reached the threshold.

The acolyte bowed, turned on his heel, and left.

"Will he tell them when the obedience powder fades?" Kirth asked.

"Doubtful," Tinge led them through the door. "His memory will be vague, with kind feelings towards me. Regardless, his self-preservation sense ought to still his tongue."

"Let's not test that by lingering," Kirth murmured.

A friendly moon welcomed them, beckoning from high above. Its beam shone on the steps leading out to the field. Marra gasped in relief, barely managing to keep from sobbing as she glanced back over her shoulder. No sign of pursuit.

If Kratchett was right...if Tryst was here....

Kirth steadied herself on the door. She, too, must be affected by their narrow escape. Marra watched the elder's hand grasp the latch - and jerk away.

"Show no doubt or fear, little Marra," Tinged whispered. "Walk shrouded in the power of Agben."

Straightening her shoulders, Marra did.

Her eyes adjusted, able to see the groups of Terrin clustered around small campfires. The population seemed to have increased tenfold since they'd first entered the Black Tower.

"Tryst," Marra whispered to Kirth. "Kratchett said he was here."

At the bottom of the steps, the woman stumbled again. Marra shored her up.

"Who is this Tryst?" Tinge asked, and Marra suddenly worried how much to say. She'd already been too free with her speech.

"A friend. Though how he could be here...."

Kirth swayed again. Thankfully Tinge grasped her other arm, for Marra sagged beneath her full weight. "My friend, are you ill?"

The elder collapsed.

Tinge lowered her, gently settling her in the soft moss. "Kirth?"

Her face glistened in the moonlight. Marra touched it - to find her skin clammy, warm. Too warm.

"Did she grab the door handle?"

Marra stared at the Terrin.

"Marra! Did she grab...."

Unable to find her voice, Marra nodded.

Tinge lifted the elder easily, cradling her as a mother might a child. And strode on.

By the Great Goose, what was happening to Kirth?

Realizing she was being left behind, Marra sprang up to follow.

"The Terrin are a dichotomy," Tryst told Jason softly. "There's a chance they would refuse to obey the Tower, yes. But if they do battle us...."

The Defense Master was staring at something behind him. "I believe," he whispered, "That we have found our Rain."

Leaning back, Tryst shifted to follow Jason's eyes.

In the moonlight he saw the two figures traveling away from the Tower. The one in the lead was undoubtedly Terrin, carrying something in its arms.

A tiny figure trailed behind, and though it wore trousers, it was feminine. Long hair fell down her back, yet not so long as a Skullan female. Nor did she move with that Agben swagger. Perhaps the Terrin had altered that.

Yet she did move straight ahead, not from a lack of fear, but from her intent to hide it. Those set shoulders and steady gaze were all too familiar.

Tryst was on his feet before Jason could stop him.

When he reached her his hand shot out, grabbing her arm. He felt her start, sensed her terror.

"Marra, it's me."

Her face tilted up to him. Her eyes squeezed shut, slowly opened. And then she sagged so that if he hadn't held her, she'd have fallen.

"Marra?"

"He said you were here." Her voice trembled. "I didn't see how...." Her free hand lifted, not to push away as he half expected, but to clutch his other arm. Her eyes glistened in the moonlight - tears?

Tryst breathed in relief - she was *glad* to see him. However she got here, she wasn't hiding it. She wasn't betraying anyone.

Beyond her, the Terrin turned, and he realized it

was Kirth that it carried. The creature eyed him balefully.

"You, skin," it rasped out. "Be you the one called Tryst?"

For an instant - just a blink of the sun - Marra wanted to throw her arms around Tryst, cling to him as a person fallen into the sea at Mid Isle would cling to a rescuing rope.

She hadn't believed Kratchett. She hadn't seen how it could be possible.

When Tinge turned round, Kirth unconscious and pale in her grasp, Marra took a deep breath and took hold of herself.

"Kirth's ill," she told him. "We need to tend her."

Tryst turned, pointing the way. "We're over here."

The Prince led them past several camps, skirting Terrin clusters before veering towards a group near the goss forest. She felt Tinge halt behind her.

"I cannot..." the Terrin rasped.

"Marra!"

Drail stood up, looking as astonished as she felt. Beside him sat Manten, Olver, Old Merle...and Jason.

She spun to face the reluctant Terrin. "They're friends," she told her. "We're safe. These are my friends."

Tinge's fangs grew short in a grimace. For the blink of the sun the Agben elder remained still.

Before Marra could urge her further, Tinge squared

her massive shoulders and marched after Tryst.

Thus following her, Marra witnessed the wave of astonishment that rippled through the Terrin in the camp.

A large Terrin near the fire leapt to his feet, eyes riveted on Tinge. "Woman?!" he cried. "You approach us here?!"

Tinge plucked out her Agben necklace, the dove with the sparkling blue eyes, and held it out for all to see.

"Lady!" All Terrin around the campfire rose and fell to their knees, as Skullan would before King Bactor. Every single one.

"We approach on the Agben path," Tinge declared, in a voice ringing with all the authority of a Queen. "We seek your assistance."

"You have that and all that you wish," the large Terrin said, and stood. His hand flew out before him, as if he caught a biteme as it wandered by. Yanking the fist to his chest, it slapped against his fur as he bowed his head once more. "I am Qwall, Leader. By Yute's own luck, your path has led you to the strongest male."

The Agben Terrin inclined her head, turning back to Marra. And though the firelight made it difficult to be certain, she thought Tinge rolled her eyes.

At last Marra had Kirth settled on a sleep-sling spread on the ground. Tinge had commanded their own fire, and Qwall's Terrin swiftly built it.

The elder Skullan's skin seemed paler, her breath rasping in her throat. Kirth was worsening before her eyes.

Behind her Tryst and Drail stood, and a tall blond female who appeared rather quickly when Drail had hugged Marra in welcome.

"What is wrong with Kirth?" Marra asked Tinge.

"There are rumors of...distrust...within Zaria. The Tower door cannot be opened from without, as you saw. And from within...an odd tale describes a poison applied to the handle at nightfall. To catch the unwary."

"What sort of poison?" Marra felt Kirth's cheek and forehead. Her body temperature was climbing.

"I do not know," Tinge frowned, also touching Kirth's skin. "Until tonight I thought it just a foolish story."

Carefully Marra grasped the sick woman's wrist, turning her hand upright. Leaning over, she sniffed the palm. "Kwitt," she told the Terrin. "Some of this smells like the sleeping potion Rain used. But - there's other ingredients. Other odors."

She hoped to see recognition in Tinge's eyes. Instead the Terrin gaped, mouth open, fangs glistening with moisture.

"Kirth said you could smell things far better than most skins. But I never believed...."

"She's fading," Marra broke in. "Tinge, what do we

do?"

"Child, I do not know."

Tinge rocked back on her heels, staring down at the elder skin. For the first time in many years, horror prickled her spine.

Kirth was not just an old friend - she was Agben. There existed a sacred bond, a trust that Terrin Agben would honor and protect the skins of the sisterhood sent to them. This exchange of ideas, sharing of knowledge, had pledged the two races to the Agben way for more than five centuries.

And here, now, *she* was breaking that trust. It must not be.

For the first time, she saw value in the skin's methods. Terrin learned exactly what they wished, never bothering to play with that which didn't appeal. Yet if she'd learned as a skin, she would have studied healing first.

She might have had the tools to save Kirth.

Wildly her mind spun, seeking a path out of this maze.

"Marra, lend me your herbs."

The little skin with the big eyes stared at her, before reaching for her belt. "You know the cure?" her soft voice pleaded.

Tinge shook her head. "I'm making more Obedience Paste. Someone in that tower must know a counter to it."

After a moment, the skin girl nodded. But Tinge knew she held little hope in her heart.

"Marra, do what you can," she added softly. "If this smell reminds you of something you once cured, perhaps it will help again."

Marra's gaze held that wide-eyed fright of a skin, like a tiny mikmouse drowning in an unexpected pool. Tinge waited for the bleating fears of the novice, of the hairless. And was surprised by the child's self-possession.

"I'll do all I can," Marra whispered.

All that night Marra worked.

The potion that saved King Bactor seemed to slow Kirth's fading health, though no more. She tried a stronger variant, using two Trevor seeds, without visible affect.

And realized further attempts must wait. Kirth herself had warned against plying the King with too much too fast.

How she wished she could ask the elder's advice now.

For three long days she worked, neither sleeping nor eating more than might be snatched at the sick woman's side. Kirth, who had always appeared larger than life, seemed to shrink before her eyes.

Tinge's obedience paste failed. Not that the acolyte who opened the door at her rap didn't bleat out all he knew - but he knew nothing that would help.

Someone, the Agben Terrin felt certain, did know the counter. But that someone was too high up for access.

On the third day Tinge stood beside her, insisting she eat a grain ball. "Child, you need your own health to help another. Yute favors success when all is done - not half." Tryst had been feeding her the things for three days, ignoring her protests. In truth, she was weary of them.

The Terrin laid the furry side of her paw to Kirth's white cheek. "Your brew wants to work," she told Marra. "This poison is just too stubborn."

"You can tell that by touching her?"

Tinge nodded. "The energy stirs within her - but can't quite overset the evil threads."

It was the phrasing that hatched the idea. "Tinge," she asked slowly. "Do you have any of that Obedience Paste leftover?"

"Twill take but a blink of the sun to make."

"What do you think will happen if we rub it on Kirth?"

The Agben Terrin sat back on her heels. "I do not know."

"Is it possible this poison is Agben? Third discipline, I mean."

Tinge stared at her for long, long blinks of the sun before speaking. "There are deadly poisons that require no Agben influence, girl. But it is possible - quite possible - that Zaria would wish to control this poison. Stave off the affects, so they might discover what the victim's purpose was in leaving."

The Terrin's fangs grew short, then long, in a way Marra found fascinating.

"Yes," she said slowly. "I would guess it possible."

Marra nodded. "The aroma of the Kwitt, and other things, points that way. If that is so, would adding the Obedience Paste to this mix counter whatever ingredient forces her body to fail?"

Again Tinge stared. Marra could only hope it wasn't because she thought her crazy.

"Not a paste," Tinge finally spoke. "I'll brew the proper Reeder potion."

And that was what she did.

Marra tried applying that to the elder's skin, both under the nose and on the palm. The effect, if effect it had, was slight.

At last she did as Tinge urged, and placed it on Kirth's tongue. First by itself, and finally, mixed with the healing potion.

Kirth opened her eyes the next morning. "What...Marra? Child, what happened to me?"

A surge of emotion welled up in her throat. She couldn't speak.

So Tinge told her.

Pinter sighed.

He was disappointed not to find Bowag in the counsel room or in his suite. Disappointed, but not surprised. More and more often, the High Priest of

Zaria, Master of the Tower, strolled the parapet.

Pinter climbed the remaining stairs to the twelfth level and passed the sealed doors of the Scroll room. He slipped into the alcove just beyond, set such that no one without prior knowledge would notice it.

The stairs here spiraled, and were even narrower than those of the dungeon. They always made him feel clumsy. His fingers grasped the edge of the carved niche that served as a hand railing. So shallow was the niche that he sometimes wondered if Zaria had been built by the skins.

That was blasphemy, of course. Few skins had ever seen this tower, and only four from the inside.

Reaching the thirteenth level, a level most priests were unaware existed, Pinter shoved against the thick portal and stepped out into the sunshine.

The parapet circled the column, offering views in all directions. A tiny roof offered shelter to those standing on it, the covering not quite reaching the edge by the railing. Supposedly acolytes once stood guard here, watching those who passed or approached, allowing Zaria to prepare for whatever came its way. Pinter himself had once served here.

Bowag had changed that, due, so he claimed, to a profound vision from a counsel of the stones. But if that were so, Yute's reasons stayed well hidden.

Pinter suspected many of Bowag's visions arose more from selfish whim than divine guidance. But suspicions were one thing; voicing them was something else entirely.

In truth, serving Bowag had come to remind him of the story of the Terrin catching a darop by the tail. The moral being that half a plan - how to sneak up and grab the thing - was useless without the other half - how to escape with all one's fur.

He'd followed Bowag without question for so long. The closer he got to the High Priest, the more he doubted the Terrin's motives.

The more he doubted the Terrin's sanity.

Yet having walked this path deep into a tangled jungle, he now saw no other trail out.

Bowag stood at the railing, surveying the Gathering field.

"We ordain and they come," he waved at the Terrin below. "See, Pinter? They obey without hesitation."

"The Agbens have escaped the dungeons," Pinter told him, wincing at the satisfaction in his own voice.

The High Priest remained by the rail, eyes wandering the scene below. For a blink of the sun, Pinter doubted he'd fully understood.

Then, "How?"

"One of the acolytes appears to have freed them. He died opening the Tower door at night."

"Death should not come for hours."

"It seems we have too few here to properly walk the guard routes. He was not discovered until it was too late to question him." Pinter had known that for some time, though the fault lay in recruitment, not guard duty. Over the last decade the number of eager new acolytes had dwindled - likely due to some of Bowag's own innovations.

But that, too, was not something he could safely mention.

"Could our Agben skin have done this?"

"A natural thought," Pinter inclined his head. "But I do not think so. Rain is far more interested in her own power than any other consideration. And I do not think she likes the other Agben. She certainly does not like the other skins."

"We shall address the Gathering. Set them to seeking the fugitives."

Pinter shook his head, quickly stopping himself before Bowag could take offense. "Agben females are highly revered, Wisdom. I'm not sure they will give her to us against her will. Remember," he added quickly, before the other could voice his usual objections, "we have kept ourselves isolated for some time, while Agben is perceived to have always served. Most will lack the...wisdom...to blindly obey."

Bowag was silent for some time. Alarmed, Pinter could do nothing but wait.

"Gather the inner circle," the High Priest finally told him. Pinter bowed and left as fast as he could without losing all his dignity.

When he saw the skin woman marching up the stairs, Pinter almost ducked into a room. The last thing he needed was more of her whining. He didn't, because running from a female - let alone a skin - was beneath him.

"The dungeon cells are empty," Rain hissed. "Did you move the prisoners without telling me?"

"They managed an escape," he said, watching her face carefully. "Bowag wonders if you helped your Agben friends."

"Don't be ridiculous," she spat, eyes flashing even in the dim light. "They must be found! They cannot be allowed to go free."

She was as short-sighted as Bowag, he thought, though perhaps with more reason. After all, Rain had never seen the interaction between male and female Terrin.

"Don't be ridiculous," he hissed.

7.

THE SUN HAD BARELY breached the horizon when Tryst accepted a fragrant tea from Jason. They sat by the remnants of last night's campfire, surveying the furry mounds of sleeping Terrin. So many had come that Tryst couldn't tell where the one village's snoring citizens ceased and another's began.

He'd always assumed the Terrin population was few. His grandsire had declared them both rare and shy; and old tales told on the Great Continent hinted they might be dying out. Now he wondered if such tales grew from mere rumor or a deliberate misdirection.

Movement caught his eye. Squinting against the glint of dawn, he spied a small figure slipping quietly around the camp, to stop by Kirth's sleep-sling. Marra, looking so odd in the breeches. To think she'd traveled across the desert continent in her skirts.

She stood with arms folded beneath her breast, gazing down at her patient.

"Marra," he called softly. Too softly, he thought, yet she looked up. And made her way towards him.

"Would you like a cup of tea?" he asked when he noticed the purple smudges under her eyes. Before she could answer Jason rose, offering her his steaming cup.

"I'll get another." The defense master bowed and left.

She hesitated.

"Sit and drink," Tryst smiled.

Cradling the cup, she gracefully lowered beside him.

"Marra, how did you get here?"

"Me?" she gasped, staring at him. She then sipped her tea, as if gathering her words. "When Drail did not want me to travel, Kirth took me. Agben is on both continents. We meet with our sister here...annually, I think."

"And when the Terrin was revealed, fled the city, they didn't think to inform the Crown?"

He watched her brows draw down, her lips purse. "I believe Agben had sworn to keep the secret. Not many of the sisters even know."

"Did you know?"

"I'm a mere student! The first I knew of this was stepping into Tinge's garden."

Of course she wouldn't know of Agben's traditions. Relieved, he touched her arm.

"You," she glared, "let me believe Drail had decided he didn't need me."

A protest rose to his lips - but he realized she spoke truth. Drail couldn't tell her because he'd sworn him to secrecy.

Tryst had been angry at the gamesman, seemingly abandoning her in a comet game, leaving her behind with that look on her face. He'd wanted Drail to make her feel better, to offer some pretty lie. But Drail would not dishonor her by lying. Only Tryst could have spoken to ease her hurt that day. And he'd just stood by.

"I am sorry, Marra." Perhaps his sincerity came through, for she lost her frown. "It was deemed secret. Of course we couldn't take you."

She nodded. "I wouldn't have been of use."

"You'd have been extremely useful! I couldn't put you in danger," he corrected.

"And you feared Agben's involvement."

She was no fool, he admitted. "Yes. They come into this tale in too many places. But I trusted you - even with my father's life."

And when her eyes flew to his, seeking to confirm the truth, he smiled.

"Let me tell you all that has occurred. I would value

your insight."

And despite her astonishment, he did just that.

Marra sat quietly as Tryst told her about his grandsire's treaty, about Creesby and the gate. Until the Gathering was called before its time, he'd found no real sign of any plot.

She told him of Tinge, and the false tower where they were welcomed as friends of Rain by junior acolytes. And the tiny scrolls declaring 'the war is upon us' and 'we will return when the Trumen are gone'.

Tryst stared in astonishment. "Our Rain has been very busy."

She nodded. "Kirth is here to follow her trail."

"To discover all she's done? Or to find Rain herself?"

Marra grinned. "We did find her - she's in the Tower."

The Prince gaped. And in a blink of the sun, beckoned to someone behind her.

The Defense Master sat a moment later, his mug steaming with fresh poured tea. He frowned several times as she retold her tale.

"Rain...and Kratchett?" he hissed when she finished.

Marra nodded. "He knew Tryst were here. I didn't believe him until I saw you. He said - he begged - for you to pardon him. In exchange he'll tell you their plans. And give the layout of the Tower, I think."

"Why would he do that?" Jason growled. She noted

Tryst's quick gesture, commanding the man to control himself. Thinking her timid of the man's temper. But after dwelling in a dungeon for some days, she found the Defense Master's gruff ways no longer threatening.

"I think he doesn't like what he knows. Rain relishes her role, but Fox Boots...he's scared."

"What do you think it means?" Tryst looked at Jason.

"Likely the man was well-paid to do what he did. Perhaps the pay has ceased...or lost its luster."

"Skullan coin would be useless if Skullan civilization were gone," the Prince murmured.

"But...." Marra gasped, trying to understand. "It's Trumen who are in danger. Skullan far outnumber us."

Jason shook his head. "If Terrin speak of the race war, I doubt they are mere spectators. If they allow the two sides to fight - destroying what then remains would be easy."

As the sun climbed higher, the Terrin and gamesmen woke.

Tryst finished his solo practice. He'd preferred to practice defense drills, but knew it might rouse suspicion.

He saw Marra kneeling by a sitting Kirth, offering her a hot drink. Across the way Drail stood to stretch, smiling as Adeena joined him. The two talked softly.

Marra's eyes narrowed when she noticed the pair.

Tryst strode to her.

"Adeena is our guide," he explained. "We had to hire her out of Creesby, to pass the gates."

Adeena touched Drail's arm, guiding him towards the teakettle. Raising her eyebrows, Marra said, "We came a different way."

"Men sometimes...." Tryst failed to find the right words. He relaxed when the small smile curved her lips.

"They do," she murmured.

"You are not...concerned?"

She gave him an odd look. "Concerned?"

"Jealous," Tryst prodded.

Marra stared at him. "Jealous? I'm just his Brista."

Tryst studied her face carefully. Those deep blue eyes held nothing back. "Drail likes you. Very much."

She shrugged. "But not *that* way. No one will ever want a mere desert girl." And before he could respond, she rose and strode away.

Marra honestly believed that - he'd read sincerity in her eyes. She was very calm about it.

And with all the emotions stirred by her words, Tryst realized his grandsire had been right all along. The old man had never been afraid of Marra trying to entrap a prince. He'd recognized Tryst's own feelings towards a little Trumen nobody.

Apparently three days had passed.

Drail had lost count after Marra appeared out of

nowhere, but Olipp had not. The leader approached as he finished his breakfast of grain balls and tea.

Towering over them, red sparkles snapping the surrounding air, Olipp growled, "Have you recovered enough to meet my challenge?"

Drail managed to swallow his drink before nodding.

"After the noon meal digests," the Terrin rumbled, and spun on his heel. "We shall chance our play."

Adeena, perched on a log, beamed at him. "You lack no courage, Drail Gamesman. Olipp's confident of Yute's favor."

"I am confident of my skill," Drail grinned.

"Now you play Terrin?" a familiar voice asked. Marra approached, peeping round from behind him.

"'Tis why we're here," he told her with a glance at Adeena.

He felt relief as her open lips stilled, pressing together.

"Brave skins, to stand near the darop cone," the guide smiled.

"Darop cone?" Marra asked. And looked at him.

"Rules," he sighed, "are somewhat different on the Dim Continent."

Marra watched the men stretch.

Drail, with the sweat already glistening on his shoulders, joking with Manten. Olver, smiling grimly at whatever the two said. She'd seen it many times, although the tension felt higher.

And Tryst, speaking softly with Jason as he eased one leg into his hamstring stretch. She hadn't seen Tryst with the team since the first game in the Black Arena.

Preparing to face Terrin when they'd yet to beat a Skullan team. On a giant field of moss, with the cone guarded by poisoned teeth. Drail hadn't even wanted the Birr Elixir - or he had, but changed his mind when Tryst whispered something in his ear.

Marra jumped at the girl guide's voice. "This is their third game."

Adeena joined her, beaming proudly at the gamesmen. "They are brave, these skins. Very brave."

"They have already faced two Terrin teams?"

The blond nodded. "Acquitted themselves well."

"They won?"

Adeena sneered at her. "Of course not."

Four Terrin approached from across the field, mountainous creatures striding in that awkward gait. Fangs gleaming, as if they salivated at the chance to sink into hairless flesh.

Of course not, Marra realized.

Jason approached, jovially setting an arm around her shoulders, tugging her towards the men. To Adeena it would appear she was Jason's girl.

His mouth pressed into the hair covering her ear. "Marra, see if you can make anything out of this brew."

Drail drank from a waterskin, ominously colored scarlet, and passed it on to Manten. When Manten had swallowed, wiping the dredges from his mouth, he handed it to her.

"No, little Marra," Jason laughed aloud, while his eyes insisted she sniff it. "That drink is too potent for females."

The Terrin gamesmen laughed - at least, she thought it laughter - as she held the opening under her nose.

A familiar odor assailed her - of earth and grass, with that horrid layer of charred flesh beneath. Kwitt. That ingredient Rain had used to alter the appearance of a Terrin.

A single drop remained on the lip of the waterskin - her finger caught it before she passed the thing to Tryst. Dared she taste it?

Eyes locked with hers, the Prince lifted the thing, drinking despite her quick head shake. And handed it on to Olver.

Without conscience thought, she stuck the captured drop in her mouth. The Kwitt aroma tripled on her tongue - along with a different, more subtle taste. Different, yet familiar. Evoking images of the Agben School, of slipping in through one of the hidden entrances.

Wiskett Bramble. The potent vine by the doorway that Leah said held no purpose.

Tryst watched her carefully - but she couldn't say anything with Adeena nearby. With the tiniest nod, she gestured it likely wouldn't kill him.

What it would do, she had no clue.

A Terrin with a white cloth tied on its arm appeared by the tooth ring, dropping comet balls upon the moss. The Terrin surrounded by the red dust - she didn't know what else to call it - shuffled out to join him. Drail did the same.

Marra turned toward Tinge and Kirth, but Jason held her firmly in place. To maintain the pretense, she decided, and slipped out from his arm altogether.

"Come," she smiled as Leah would smile at her beau Fallon. Grabbing the defense master's hand, she hauled him along after her.

She took a seat next to Kirth. After a blink of a sun, he sat beside her.

"Kirth," Marra asked quietly. "What is that red dust surrounding that Terrin?"

The elder shook her head.

"Halo," Tinge rumbled. "Males feel the need to distinguish themselves from time to time."

Indeed, as Marra watched, the Terrin seemed to swell before her, looming larger on the field. The one called Olipp towered over the shrinking Terrin judge.

To her astonishment, she realized Drail also swelled in size. Not to Terrin gamesmen proportions, but his head was now above the shoulder of the smaller Terrin judge.

"Stars," Jason gasped.

Marra rubbed her eyes and looked again. Truly, the judge looked smaller. And even as she pondered this,

Kirth stared at her.

"By the Great Goose, child. I believe you've grown larger."

Tryst strode across the field, flanked by Manten and Olver.

The waterskin drink had tasted odd, and unlike the Birr Elixir he felt...something. Different. As the Terrin approached, he realized he found them less intimidating. Smaller somehow.

No - for Olipp loomed larger than ever beside the tiny judge. Yet the nervous qualms at the sheer size of the creatures did not rise from his gut as they had the first game.

A bark rang out. The Terrin sprang into action, and Drail sprang with them.

Immediately Olipp shot for the cone; immediately Drail jumped to block him. Drail missed, though Tryst couldn't see how. His aim seemed perfect.

Olipp's aim had also appeared true - yet the ball sailed over the teeth and beyond.

Shaking himself, Tryst launched toward another Terrin with a ball. He leapt to intercept its shot.

The sphere hit not his hands but his forearm. He barely managed to catch it, stumbling slightly before sprinting toward the teeth.

A Terrin raced to block him. Tryst shot past, intending to graze the hairy thing to break its balance. Yet he missed, feeling nothing but air.

Drail sprang up from one angle; Olipp from another. Tryst took his shot -

- and the Terrin caught it. And spun, galloping toward the teeth. The crowd reaction told him the comet was sunk.

Manten sped across the field, another ball in his grasp. He aimed -

- and was trampled from behind by a Terrin who halted immediately, as if *concerned* for an injured skin.

Even as Tryst digested this, Olipp sunk a second comet. The game, barely begun, was over.

Running to the fallen gamesmen, he was still the last to arrive. The Terrin - all four of the Terrin - were already there, staring down anxiously.

"Is he alive?" Olipp rumbled softly, as Drail checked the man's pulse.

"At the moment."

Marra was hauling Kirth to her feet when the Terrin bore Manten across the field.

"Fools," the elder mumbled beneath her breath. It would have been better to leave him where he'd fallen until Kirth examined him. Drail and Tryst knew this - but they'd failed to convey the information to Olipp.

Marra spread a sleep-sling on the moss, and observed as the injured man was gently laid upon it. No limbs hung awkwardly at least, though he winced when his head touched the ground.

Kirth ran hands over his arms and legs, felt his

forehead, rested palms on his chest. "Can you hear me, gamesmen?"

His head moved slightly, stopped. "Yes," he gasped.

"What do you feel? Pain or confusion?"

"I feel both," Manten opened his eyes. Marra worried until he grinned at Drail. "Did we win?"

Olipp threw back his head and howled with what, she was sure, was Terrin laughter.

That evening Marra had good news for Drail. "Manten is bruised," she explained. "But no serious damage anywhere. He could play in two days, if that was necessary. If not, four would be better."

The Leader of the Hand of Victory sat by a fire that Marra had carefully watched being made. A sprinkling of powder had been added to the wood, resulting - she was sure - in a less heated flame. Perfect for a warm night.

On first glance she'd thought the Terrin of the Dim Continent primitive, but they used Agben studies to do many things that had never occurred to those in Missea. She was no longer sure who was truly the more advanced.

"Thank you," Drail smiled. "Sit, Marra. Tell me how you came to be here."

Beyond their fire - beyond several fires - two robed figures moved through the Gathering. They spoke to one group, causing a sort of stir, before stepping on to the next.

"You have been working since you came, healing Kirth or Manten," Drail added. "We haven't had a chance to swap stories."

"Kirth brought me...."

Tinge and Qwall loomed up, blocking her view of the two figures. "Marra, lay down beside Kirth. And cover yourself with a sleep sling," Tinge hissed. "Now."

"The other skins?" Qwall murmured, as she hurried off to obey.

"All know they are here," Tinge told him. "Best to let them be seen."

She felt Drail stir, leaping to his feet. "What is happening?"

"See that the girl - both women - are hidden," Qwall told him.

Her sleep-sling unfurled, Marra dropped down beside Kirth, tugging the cloth over them. Then she held still, hardly daring to breath.

"Marra?" Kirth asked sleepily.

"We must be still and silent," she whispered back.

Peeking from beneath the sling, she saw three Terrin approach. At least they wore no robes. Their quiet conversation was difficult to hear - words like 'skin' and 'tower' stood out, but the linking phrases were lost in the night. For an instant the Terrin loomed closer.

And then dispersed. Whatever they'd told Qwall, they were not searching the camp.

Waiting, her nerves trembling through her body, she gasped aloud when Tinge approached. The Agben sat very close, sipping from a steaming mug, and motioned Marra to stay when she would have sat up.

"It seems," she spoke quietly, "that we have a problem."

From beneath her covering, Marra saw two boots emerge from the nearby trees. Too far to see the fox mark, but she knew it was there none-the-less.

"You do indeed," Kratchett said.

Tryst was chomping at the bit by the time he finally got to question Kratchett.

To think he'd traveled so far to find this traitor, only to watch him calmly sit across a campfire. Qwall, however, insisted on waiting till most of the Gathering slept. And, he realized in surprise, Qwall's village also slept. Either they didn't know what was happening, or they didn't want to know.

With Drail and Jason flanking Tryst, Qwall took a place beside Tinge.

"The Tower seeks the missing skins," the Terrin leader growled softly. "The priests instruct they are to be found and returned."

"But...the others *know* we're here," Marra said softly. She and Kirth had finally been allowed to sit up, hunkering behind the two Terrin so their forms would not be visible to stray eyes.

"The Tower is feared rather than trusted," Tinge

rumbled. "And with the brave gamesmen skins already winning approval, they are hesitant."

"So they will protect us," Kirth sighed.

"Let us say rather, they prefer not to be involved."

"How safe are they - we - precisely?" Tryst looked to Qwall.

The creature's shoulders rose and fell in the shrugging gesture. "All is...unprecedented. A Gathering between Gathering times; shaka skins challenging Terrin. Tower priests roaming among us, making demands. It is unsettling."

"You can give them this skin," Jason turned to Kratchett.

Tryst watched the prisoner's face, looking for any hint of cunning or guile. Instead, he would swear, there was naught but fear.

"They push the race war," Kratchett spoke hoarsely. "The Black Tower plots to stir it, to set it off. They think it will eliminate vast numbers of us."

"Eliminate Trumen?" Jason frowned. "Or do they intend to support them against the Skullan?"

Kratchett shook his head. "They do not distinguish between us at all."

"Then...." Jason exchanged a look with Tryst.

"Eliminate skins," Tryst realized even as he spoke the thought aloud. "They care not which side survives. They care not if either side survives."

Kratchett nodded frantically. "In truth few inside the Tower know the plot. They had intended to question the Prince, to learn much about the skin numbers and capabilities. To learn about their ways. When King Bactor was taken instead, they were far less organized. Less prepared."

"An awful lot of trouble just for information."

"Remember they do not like to leave the continent. Keeping him here would have been a sort of backup plan."

"And you were happy to help," Drail accused.

The man frantically shook his head. "I was paid by one Skullan to transport another. The Terrin influence revealed itself the night I fled Missea."

Tryst fell silent, pondering. Fox Boots, as Marra called him, could not be trusted, yet somehow he believed the man. But exactly where that led....

"This makes no sense," Tinge broke the quiet. "We have no need to conquer other lands. We have no need to destroy other life forms. Terrin are shy. Most spend an entire lifetime never seeing a skin."

"I do not fear *skins*," Qwall rumbled.

Tryst studied him. "But you fear priests?"

It was Tinge who answered. "Tower priests tend to stay in the Tower. Only the acolytes travel among the villages. And those less frequently these days."

"We have not seen a Tower robe in two Gatherings," Qwall told her.

"Ten years," Tryst breathed.

"They say recruitment is down," Kratchett told them quietly. "New acolytes are rare - no one wants to enter the Tower. Some say it is the fault of the head priest - obsessed with his own schemes."

Qwall rumbled, eying Tinge. "Agben has always been available. They heal, they provide useful mixtures. They do not travel often, but their places of residence are known. I can speak to a lady within three days - and can depend on her aid without fear of denial.

"The Tower," the Terrin stopped speaking to glance around. Not wanting to be being overhead, Tryst decided. "The Tower is here only. One approaches with offerings in hand, begging for whatever is sought. There is little to be gained from the priests these days."

"Yet the Gatherings are here," Jason pointed out.

Qwall nodded. "They have always been here. When I was young, the priests would bless it, move among us. Some boys would follow them into the Tower, choosing the priest training. Then, before I was Leader, boys had to approach the Tower on their own, as no one came out.

"Now no one approaches. Instead we pretend the Tower doesn't exist."

"I need to read the scrolls," Tinge decided.

"But lady, you cannot get to them," Qwall rasped.

"Then they will have to be brought to me."

Tryst knew before the next words followed. Not because he understood the Tower workings, nor did he see the plan. He knew, he realized with a sinking heart, because it seemed inevitable she'd once again have to step into danger.

"Marra," Tinge turned to face her. "You must return to the Tower."

"Me?"

Marra stared across the small blaze of the fire. At Kirth, who seemed to nod her head and wince simultaneously. At Drail, who stared at Tinge as if the Agben had spoken another language.

And at Tryst, whose face in the flickering light mirrored her own shock. "Cannot Tinge go?" he frowned. "Hidden in a robe?"

Qwall's fangs drew longer - open-mouthed, Marra realized. "Females cannot be males."

"We...." Tinge turned to look at her. "We *feel* different, my friends. As surely as your nose finds Kwitt, male Terrin could not be fooled. A robe would cloak nothing."

Marra wondered again just how this Terrin feeling worked. Was it more than a sort of empathy?

"What matter the scrolls?" Kratchett hissed. "Things are as they are regardless."

"The Black Tower and High Priest are very powerful," Tinge explained. "Terrin might not like what they say, but outright disobedience would be very difficult. If, however, they have lied...broken from the true scrolls...."

Marra caught Tryst's confusion. "Tinge remembers

different teachings," she explained.

"Could you not dress a male Terrin as a priest?" Drail asked.

Qwall actually shuddered.

"There are protocols, ways things are done. He would be exposed far too easily. Whereas a female skin -"

"Rain." Marra sighed. Stars, she didn't want to go back inside that dark structure. "They wouldn't see that I'm Trumen?"

"Doubtful," Tinge smiled. "We see naked skin, hairless face, tiny bodies. The subtleties between Skullan and Trumen escape us."

Part of her waited, hoping for a counter to the logic. Hoping for Tryst to stop it, she realized. Looking at his eyes, she knew he very much wanted to.

Just as she knew he could not.

Looking at the sky, Kratchett judged it maybe three hours till dawn. At that time the Tower activity would quicken, and they'd never make it out.

He knew, as soon as the subject was broached, he'd be risking his neck. Try as he might - and he tried very hard - no alternative occurred. He couldn't even abandon the girl inside; if he dared return without her they'd never set him free, no matter what story he told. And his chances of surviving the Dim jungle without help weren't good.

So he led her through the goss forest, slipping

round to the far side of the Tower. And, brushing clear the canopy of vines and leaves, swung up the metal ring. This back entrance was known to only three priests - Rain certainly had no suspicion.

But then Rain hadn't lived a life where escape routes meant survival.

It took both his hands to lift it.

Throwing off the robe she'd wrapped herself in to hide her skirts, Marra gasped.

"Keep quiet," he hissed. "Previously no guards were set here at night, but that might easily have changed."

Some at the campfire had preferred waiting, planning, and Kratchett had done his best to support that. The Prince had declared, however, that there was little to plan and much 'to be lost. And once his task became obvious, Kratchett preferred to get it over with. Any day now he expected the priests to come seeking him.

He doubted Rain was as safe as she believed.

The steps lay half buried in moss and dead leaves, rendering them treacherous. But the girl shied away from his offered hand.

Lowering the heavy door was the most difficult part. He decided to leave it open.

"No one will see this," he said when she stared. At least, not till dawn. Besides, opening it from the inside was very hard - and they might be in a hurry.

He descended, hoping she'd follow.

As always, two torches blazed at the bottom. He

grasped the one and trotted along the tunnel.

Glancing over his shoulder, he saw her little face set, her lower lip between her teeth. But she never hesitated.

He had to admit, she had courage.

Marra had thought it would be easier, entering beyond the shadow of the Tower. She couldn't see the dark fog oozing from its walls at night, and slipping inside through an entrance shrouded by trees sounded much more pleasant.

But traveling through the goss woods in her skirt was challenging. It took much effort to keep the material free of Reeders and their trailing web. She found she missed the silly trousers.

Watching Kratchett yank up the iron ring in the dirt, seeing the dimly lit tunnel that reminded her of a fresh-dug grave, she shivered.

The slick steps led down into the earth between walls covered with slime, forcing her to tread carefully so as not to touch anything. If her guide had been Tryst or Drail this would have been so much easier.

Instead she relied on an enemy to guide her.

Marra hesitated by the second torch. It would offer comfort to carry her own - but then the light would reveal her face. And if they chanced to find themselves fleeing later, the torch marking the way out could save their lives.

Kratchett observed her leave it without comment.

The tunnel sloped deeper into the ground. Its sides smoothed, the slime vanishing as they traveled away from the goss woods. Silence seemed to swell in her ears, urging her to break it by peppering the man ahead with questions. She refrained.

And then a door loomed out of the darkness. Kratchett cast her a quelling look - as if she'd been chattering ceaselessly the whole way - and handed her the torch.

Using both hands, he eased it open. And slipped his head around. When he pulled back he gave her a steady glare.

"Remember you are Rain, I am your servant" he hissed. "You have ordered me to light your way, and where you go is neither priest's nor Terrin's concern."

He held that glare for a blink of the sun, until she slowly nodded.

Then the door opened wide and they passed through.

Now, Marra knew, they walked beneath the Tower itself, too near those dungeon cells that haunted her dreams still. When they reach the familiar stairs she held her breath, waiting to see which direction he'd take. Up or down.

She didn't draw air again until the man was climbing up to ground level. Which was foolish - everything looked equally dark and unnerving wherever they stood.

Kratchett paused on the landing, turning to her.

"The scrolls lie on the twelfth level, in a tiny room few know how to reach. We should encounter no Terrin - but if we do, glare at them. Speak not, herb girl, for your voice is nothing like Rain's. Answer questions only with a glare, and leave the rest to me."

She nodded.

And then they climbed.

Spiraling upwards, on and on, she lost count of landings, of the levels they passed. Were they even halfway to their objective? She couldn't guess.

At one point Kratchett paused, and even as she thought they were done climbing, she saw the fear on his face. He sprinted up faster.

Marra was forced to snatch her skirts high and race after him.

Two levels later he slowed. The spiral stopped - they were at the top.

When she sighed audibly, he whirled with another glare. This might be easier, she wanted to inform him, if he treated her less like an adversary. After all, their fates this night were bound together.

She said nothing, of course.

Seemingly the passage was narrower here, and few choices presented themselves. Kratchett led her to what looked a dead end.

And then pushed hard on the wall. Nothing happened.

He shoved again, straining with effort. Just when she opened her mouth to ask, she heard the subtle click.

He stepped back as part of the wall swung open. A hidden door.

"Rain doesn't even know of this," he murmured in grim satisfaction.

They stepped through to a large circular chamber, the most pleasant by far she'd seen within this dark Tower. Many torches blazed in their brackets, brighter than those that lit the halls or entrance room. Bright enough to reveal the vivid color in the rugs, the cushioned chairs and couches. And, she realized, in tapestries.

Tapestries depicting Terrin and skins building huts such as Tinge lived in, gathering fruit, sitting round a campfire. And - she could scarcely believe it - playing comet.

One tapestry, larger than the others, showed six scenes of eating together. And in each, the Terrin number grew fewer as the skin population increased.

"Get the scrolls!" Kratchett hissed at her elbow.

Recalled to her purpose, Marra dropped her gaze to the circular shelves beneath the tapestries, and the rolls of cloth within. All her life she'd heard tales of the Zaria Scrolls, but she'd somehow imagined the term meant verbal teachings, stories carefully handed down generation to generation, just as the lore of Agben existed in the mind of the women who practiced it. The stark reality overwhelmed her.

For there wasn't one or two or three. There

appeared, literally, to be hundreds...maybe thousands.

By the Desert Crane, she could only carry an armful. How was she to choose?

"Hurry!" Kratchett hissed, stepping back to the doorway. Marra couldn't guess if he was standing guard or preparing to flee.

The oddly curved shelves rose three tiers high, then six tiers, then three, alternating round the chamber. Each stuffed full of scrolls. As she trod farther in, she saw that each three tiered-space was topped with one of the tapestries. With fifty or more scrolls on each shelf....

"Someone's coming!"

Kratchett vanished. The door swung shut.

Whirling on her heel, Marra sagged in relief to see the door hadn't quite closed. She'd been afraid of trying to figure out the secret latch.

It was then she truly noted the room's center, where a single, plush couch sat beside a low, round table. With a fancy brazier - fire ready to be lit - perched atop. Perhaps to provide even more reading light, for the room was quite warm. Beneath the brazier was an indentation.

Hurrying to it, Marra saw gold inlay intricately winding around the edge of what proved to be a deep shelf beneath the fire pit, with three scrolls tucked inside. These, unlike the others lining the walls, were wrapped with a cord of animal skin, worn and smelling faintly of treatment to keep it supple. The parchment looked very thick, indicating great age.

"My orders are to remain," Kratchett's voice broke the silence.

Snatching the scrolls, she slipped to the door.

Peering through the crack, she saw a large expanse of white robe between two hairy arms. The back of a Terrin.

"You cannot stay here," it growled.

"I cannot disobey."

Before doubt could assail her, Marra slipped out and rounded the wall, sliding into an alcove. And, meaning to back as far as she could, found not a wall but an opening.

A stairway up.

She whirled and fled.

And was welcomed by the night sky. Beneath a full moon and blanket of stars, she stood on a parapet circling the Tower top. The gray shape of the forest lay below to her right, the Gathering ground to her left. Seemingly everyone below slept.

But several did not, she knew. Tryst and Drail would be waiting, worrying. Kirth and Tinge would exude calm while stealing glances at the Tower. They all depended on her.

The idea didn't actually form as words in her head. Instead her feet scurried round to the other side, the side away from the Tower door, away from where she'd ever seen the priests.

Her hands dropped the scrolls over the railing.

And then she sped back to the stairs and down.

"I see no one here," she heard a low growl.

Reaching the alcove, Marra peeked round to see the priest on the scroll room threshold. "You lie," the Terrin rumbled.

On impulse she strode out, firm and decisive. *I am Rain*, she told herself.

"Kratchett!" she commanded, striding out to confront them both. "Come!"

The Terrin priest moved to block her path. "Why are you here?" it demanded, glaring down at her, fangs bared.

I am Agben, Marra thought, straightening her shoulders. From deep inside she found her own answering glare.

"Out of my way, oaf!" Shoving past, she marched away.

From the sound of the footsteps that quickly caught up, she knew Kratchett strode with her.

"You've stunned him," Kratchett murmured. Whether he was pleased or furious Marra couldn't guess.

When they reached the stairs, they ran.

Jason sat where he could keep an eye on the goss wood.

He hadn't liked this plan. He hadn't seen the advantage of seeking what had to be mystical writings, and he surely did not want to release a traitor to guide a very green girl. It was, as Qwall might say, risking much for little gain.

Now, with dawn bathing the dark forest in pink, chasing night shadows back to their lair, he worried what damage had been wrought.

At least the Prince still slept. Jason had begun to worry about the man's attachment to the herb waif. Smiling at Tryst's sleep bag, it gradually occurred to him that the cloth was not just still, but rather flat.

Marra sped through the dark corridor. Kratchett shot ahead like a startled desert hare, and twice she could only follow him by sound instead of sight.

At last they reached the bottom of the spiral staircase. The man paused just long enough to be sure she followed - she wondered if he'd known or cared before then.

"You don't appear to carry scrolls," he lifted his torch.

"I..."

"HALT!" a Terrin growled somewhere behind them. Kratchett loped off down the tunnel.

Marra raced after him, praying she wouldn't trip on the rough dirt floor. Keeping her eyes focused for loose rock, she never dared glance behind her, though she could hear giant feet pounding the dirt. Kratchett did look back, and what he saw scared him enough to hurl his torch at it.

The flame blinded her as he lobbed it over her head.

She tripped, tumbling to the damp soil.

From the thump and the raspy 'oof', she guessed the Terrin had also fallen. Raising her head, she saw a faint light flicker ahead.

Marra sprang up and ran.

The light became her target, her skirts in her hand as she hurtled through the void. Sounds danced dizzyingly in her ears: her feet smacking earth, her rasping breath, and the growing rumble of Terrin pursuit.

Kratchett sped up the stairs, turning just as she reached them. Able to see the steps she sprinted full out, racing up out of the tunnel into the early dawn.

And then her head was yanked backward - pain shot through her skull as she flailed helplessly off the ground.

The Terrin held her up by her long hair.

Clasping her scalp, Marra instinctively tried to lessen the pain. Her feet kicked wildly, first in reaction and then with intent. If only she could connect to its nether region....

If it *had* a nether region.

Kratchett's face loomed, gawking.

"Kick it," she gasped. The man spun and loped off into the goss forest.

Her heel landed a few pathetic bumps. The Terrin turned her, pulling her close to its glaring pupils.

"Crush," it said. And she wondered wildly if that was its threat or decision.

WHACK. Metal struck flesh, her world shook. For an instant she thought she must be dead.

And then she lay on her back, staring at a night sky warming with dawn. Her fingers worked frantically at the Terrin grasp - other fingers helped.

Tryst's face appeared, fury giving way to relief, a tiny smile. Freeing her, he plucked her up off the hoary body, turning her this way and that as if seeking bruises.

"Are you okay?" he asked.

She nodded. It was only when he frowned that she realized tears coursed down her cheeks.

He held her close, as if to comfort her. "I've got you safe."

Long moments passed before she could speak. "The scrolls."

"It doesn't matter," Tryst whispered, turning her to look into her eyes. "You're not going back."

She managed to smile. And as her tongue sought words to tell him of the scrolls, he kissed her.

Jason knew where the Prince had gone. Hurrying through the wood, he followed the trail Kratchett had taken.

He heard a metal clang before he saw them - the Terrin prone on the ground, Tryst pulling Marra free.

Sagging with relief, he smiled to himself until he caught the Prince's expression, the way he clasped the girl with a warmth not justified by unread parchment.

As if this whole mission wasn't mad enough.

And then the damn fool kissed her.

Even if he managed to bring the Heir to Missea safely back, even if they stopped the Terrin threat and saved Skullan and Trumen alike, King Bactor would not be pleased.

And somehow, Jason knew, King Ganny would blame him.

Pinter glided down the hallway toward the Scroll room.

It had been days since the Agben trio had escaped. Yet no imperious knock had rattled the Tower door; no hoard of raging women had invaded the Gathering field. Bowag now believed them safe from such outcomes.

Pinter did not.

Terrin females had a way of paying back insults, and Agben had a way of fiercely preserving life. His own mother had been Agben; she had oft told him that while the Tower called itself the seat of religion, the females with their herbs were the more spiritual. When he rose through the ranks to serve the High Priest, his mother's words came back to haunt him.

Stopping before the hidden wall, Pinter sighed. And shoved. At the audible click, he stepped back to allow the portal to swing open.

Shutting himself within, he then circled the chamber, one hand tracing the scroll shelves. He'd read many of these - writings of old priests, mostly interpreting the true Scrolls. The three Scrolls of Zaria.

Bowag insisted no one save the High Priest could unfurl the true Scrolls, nor read their words nor ponder their meaning. "You can read what the others have said," he'd been instructed. "That has always been the way."

Yet many interpretive scrolls had been scribed by mere priests, even a few acolytes, contemplating not what they'd been told third hand, but surely had read for themselves.

Pinter had already guessed, of course. He knew Bowag bent the teachings to his own purpose, enough so the Terrin barred others from reading them. Often Pinter had paced this chamber, circling the center shelf where the true Scrolls lay. Resisting the growing temptation to read the words for himself.

If he substituted one of the interpretations for a true Scroll, then even if Bowag entered the room he'd be safe.

Pinter halted, grasped the scroll nearest his hand and strode toward the center. It was time to know just how far this detour from the path had taken them all.

It was only then that he saw the Zaria scrolls were missing.

8.

KIRTH HAD TO KEEP everyone away while Tinge poured over the writings.

That is, Kirth had to keep the Prince and Defense Master away. The others proved more patient - or less eager.

Marra never pushed, of course, but hovered close by all the same. Whether the girl's own curiosity drove her or her need to appease the Prince, Kirth couldn't decide. The child actually seemed to avoid him. Perhaps she was anxious to find answers before speaking with him.

As the sun climbed the sky Tinge sat motionless, an unfurled scroll gripped in her hairy paws. The Terrin spoke not a word, but her anger was a palpable thing. It took all Kirth's years of training to keep from begging to know what she'd discovered.

The noon meal lay ready before Tinge tucked the scroll inside her traveling bag. Ponderously pushing herself off the ground, she moved to take a seat by the unlit campfire.

No one spoke a word, yet in the blink of the sun the Prince's party, together with Qwall and his Right Hand, joined her. To all appearances, merely sharing grain balls.

Tinge swallowed her food and licked her paws before speaking.

"Zaria has much to explain," she rumbled. "I have only managed the first of the three, and that with difficulty. The language is old and laden with an odd poetry - yet it is clear the text of the prophecy laid down has been altered."

"Altered?" Qwall growled.

"The Tower speaks of three wars - two that are past, and a third to come. The Priests imply these are unavoidable, even necessary. And that one race will be wiped out."

The gamesman Drail spoke up. "The Skullan have twice defeated the Trumen. Some believe the third war will end my race." And, noting the guide's confusion, he added, "We've always assumed Trumen would survive on the Wandering Continent. Skullan disdain the desert."

Kirth frowned. "When I was a young girl, it was said the third war could be avoided. Even that it would be better not to destroy Trumen. There was...an implied belief that a greater war might follow. And that Trumen could tip the balance in such a fight."

Tinge's fangs disappeared into her hairy lips. "And now no one speaks of such avoidance?"

Kirth nodded.

"Someone was trying to get a message through."

"What message?" the Prince asked calmly. Kirth found herself impressed - the boy was not the hothead she'd expect at his age.

"The first scroll describes a looming war. Weaknesses that might trigger it...even possible paths to avoid conflict."

"It does not urge battle?" The Defense Master asked casually, as if they were discussing the warmth of the afternoon.

"Emphatically, it does not."

"The Tower pushes a war its own prophecy cautions against?" The Prince stared thoughtfully at his half-eaten grain ball. "To what purpose?"

Tinge sighed, her breath whistling past her fangs. "I do not know. Perhaps the answer lies in the other scrolls." Plucking another morsel from the platter, she pushed herself upright and turned back towards her reading spot.

A wild idea occurred to Kirth. So wild, so insane that her mouth spoke before her good sense could stop it. "In the old tongue, race -"

"I must read," Tinge growled, and shuffled off.

Bowag had been slow to come.

Pinter knew the High Priest had not believed. Not because he doubted Pinter, but because he could never doubt his own assessments. The fool - yes, Pinter allowed himself to call his leader a fool - had been so sure Rain was truly his to command and control.

Now the High Priest gaped at the center shelf, at the blank space where the sacred scrolls should be.

"Shall I send for Rain?" Pinter prodded.

"She did not know where to find the room," Bowag whispered.

"The acolyte saw her and her man here last night."

"She could not do this..."

Pinter spun on his heel and strode to the door. "Fetch the Agben," he growled to the guards outside.

Rain shoved past an acolyte, striding into the counsel room. Annoyingly, it was empty.

The Gathering was full, or near enough to make no difference. Bowag claimed the escape of mere females insignificant, but then what was he waiting for? If he intended to declare war, the time was now. Before the Terrin found excuses to return home.

Pacing the room, staring at the ridiculous throne on which the High Priest so loved to pose, she worried how much Tinge and Kirth had pieced together. The Zaria Terrin disdained females, believing them dull-minded and weak of purpose.

They were fools.

Agben valued Trumen, and Kirth would never support the idea of expunging them. Tinge may not concern herself, but then she could be swayed by her old friend and that silly concept of balance.

Bowag, she strongly suspected, sat smugly on the highest level of the Tower, letting Pinter persuade him to caution. And Rain had been barred from the highest levels.

She was already marching purposefully out the door when the acolyte found her.

"Take me to Bowag," she demanded. And for once he obeyed.

Pinter met her at the top of the stairs. Twelfth level, if she'd counted correctly.

The acolyte guide left them.

"Where is Bowag?" Words trembled on her lips, ready to override his objections. He made none.

They strode down a dim hall, brought up short by a wall. Before Rain could question him, Pinter shoved against it. She heard a click - and a hidden door swung open.

Light blazed from inside, indicating the importance of the room. So much light she had to blink to clear her vision. When she could see, she gasped aloud.

A circular room, filled with color. Tapestries, numerous torches burning brightly, plush seating. Low shelving surrounded the area, packed with scrolls.

The Zaria Scrolls. She'd never dreamed there were

so many.

Bowag stood in the center, one paw resting on the raised fire pit. The other paw waved at the empty shelf beneath it.

"At last, I am to read the scrolls," Rain purred, and could not forebear a victorious smile at Pinter.

"You will return them at once," Bowag barked. "Or I will toss you from the top of this Tower."

As the afternoon wore on, Marra sat hugging her knees to chest. Gray clouds thickened, threatening to unleash a jungle downpour - a deluge so powerful it physically pounded the body. She'd seen such a rain and had no wish to see it again.

When she realized her fingers were tracing her lips, she clenched her hand and firmly dropped it to the moss.

Obviously Tryst hadn't meant anything by it. He'd simply been caught up in the moment after fighting a Terrin. She knew this; he didn't need to explain. It was fortunate Jason had interrupted them in the wood.

Speak of the devil - his boots stepped into her view. She looked up into the Defense Master's face.

"The Prince must marry when he returns to Missea," he told her.

Marra's cheeks burned.

His eyes softened. "He likes you, Marra. Just...understand. He's heir to the Skullan Empire. Already King Bactor seeks a worthy consort."

She managed a single nod before returning her gaze to his boots.

Jason may have stroked her head before retreating. Or, possibly, he merely brushed her unintentionally when he turned.

Tryst had been caught in the moment, she told herself. Foolish to make something more from a simple thing.

Out of the corner of her eye she spied the two acolytes roaming the Gathering. Probably here about the pending storm. They strode through the village camps, pausing to exchange a few words here and there while Marra tried to quiet her mind.

And then the acolytes reached Qwall, who pointed at *her*. She rose as an acolyte grabbed her arm and dragged her toward the Tower.

And then Tryst barred the way. "Release her."

He was grabbed as well.

Jason leapt up angrily; Drail and Manten quickly appeared. And when one of the robed ones seized Drail, Qwall and his entire village stood.

"By what path do you take my shaka?" he growled fiercely. So fiercely in fact that the startled acolytes fell back.

"They are skins," one gasped in surprise. Nervous surprise, Marra devoutly hoped.

Qwall stepped closer, glaring. And the men were released, though she was not.

Tryst clasped Marra's other arm. "She is Brista."

For the blink of the sun she held her breath. Then the Terrin paw withdrew, but she knew they would be back.

As the robed figures retreated toward the Tower, the heavens opened and water poured from the sky.

The jungle rain lasted a day and a night. And in all that time, Tryst couldn't think of a single decent strategy.

Many of the gathered Terrin had moved back to the trees, hanging sleep-slings and disappearing within the folds. Pummeled by torrents of water, there were few other options. Sleeping on the ground proved impossible - the cloth may be waterproof, but water ran ankle deep. One would float away or drown.

He'd watched Marra climb into her sling with ease and though he failed to imitate her movements, he had to smile. Unlike Adeena, there were no complaints from his herb girl. She was a very adaptable young woman.

They hadn't spoken since Jason had interrupted them in the woods, and Tryst hoped that adaptability would work in his favor. Surely now that she knew, she'd be patient.

He woke to a clear morning sky, a deeper blue than he'd yet seen on the Dim Continent. The air smelled fresh and felt less humid. Today might be a good day indeed.

Breaking fast with Qwall, he grinned to see Jason

striding to join them.

"This Gathering grows stale," Qwall growled. His Terrin Right Hand nodded.

"What exactly is the purpose of the Gathering?" Jason asked as he sat.

"It allows flow," the Right Hand explained. "One village has too many cooks; one has too few, so an exchange is made. This village found a new way to stitch leather and teaches others. Or a Right Hand learned of new arrivals in Creesby."

"Leaders speak," Qwall chewed his grain ball, swallowed. "We meet and share. Bigger chance for Yute to move freely through us."

"But this Gathering was...off cycle?" Jason prodded.

"Off cycle," the Right Hand echoed, and grinned in that fang-lengthening manner. "Yes, off cycle."

"A waste," Qwall grumbled. "We are summoned like children to a silent Tower. The villages grow restless...soon they will leave. We will leave."

Even as the Terrin spoke, Tryst saw the Tower door open. An ominous column of robed priests filed out.

Following his gaze, Qwall looked over his hairy shoulder. "Yute guide us. Finally."

Eight red robes and twice as many white robes emerged, lining up with the Black Tower behind them. The red robes stood in front, the white behind, with a gap in the center.

Only when the line stood complete and the Gathering fell silent did a single red-robed Terrin emerge. This one strode with authority, claiming the center spot. Tryst couldn't be sure from his distant view, but it appeared this priest used the same sparkling powder as the village leaders. No, not quite - these dancing-dust colors were both red and white.

A Terrin stepped before this leader, dipping its paw into a tiny pot and rubbing the contents on his master's throat.

"I am Bowag, High Priest of Zaria." The substance apparently made his speech much louder, for his words were easy to hear. "Yute has summoned you to hear her word. She declares the skins our enemy."

The crowd stirred with gasps and murmurs.

"They are evil. They intend to conquer Terrin, hurt Terrin. They plan to kill Terrin."

The stirring rose to startled protests.

"Skins are puny!" one voice cried. "Why would they act so foolishly?"

"How will they invade the Dim Continent?" another Terrin shouted. "They can't get past the gates of Creesby!"

"They are here now!" the priest declared, pointing at Qwall's camp. If he'd hoped to scare the Gathering, he'd failed.

They were startled, Tryst thought, but at the priest's foolishness. All the Terrin knew of Qwall's shaka. They did not fear them on the comet field - and certainly not off it.

New sounds rose. Watching Qwall's villagers, Tryst

realized they were the purring sounds of mirth.

"I brought gamesmen," Qwall stood to call to the priest. "If you fear them, I will protect you."

Now the laughter was open, and the line of priests didn't like it.

The red-robed one stepped forward, pointing at him. "Your skins have stolen the sacred scrolls of Zaria!"

Amusement died a quick death.

Qwall turned to Tryst. "Chance has led to a very bad road," he hissed softly. "We may not be allowed to protect you."

Allowed by Yute? Tryst wondered. *Or allowed by the Gathering?*

Nearby trees rustled. Tinge strode out, waving the scrolls high in the air. To Tryst's amazement, Marra and Kirth followed in her wake.

The three women marched through the Gathering unafraid, even confident. In all that time no sound was made.

Tinge mounted the small hill on which the priests stood, and the High Priest gave way to her force. Snatching the little pot from his acolyte, she rubbed its contents on her own throat.

Tryst found himself moving towards them, and was glad to see Qwall moving with him.

"The scrolls are quite safe," Tinge announced, her voice reaching the farthest ear. "Do not fear the skins, High Priest. I will protect you."

The answering fury blazing in the Terrin priest dampened the rising laughter.

Stomping his feet, Bowag roared "I need no protection!"

"Then what do you fear?" she demanded. And the entire Gathering waited to hear his answer.

Bowag's eyes rolled frantically, reminding Tryst of a cornered hare. "Yute has proclaimed their guilt."

"Not in the scrolls, Bowag of Zaria. They describe a very different danger."

Pinter watched the Agben trio, the Terrin and her two skins. They neither shouted nor threatened, yet theirs was the authority. And the more Bowag stamped his feet, the more foolish he looked. The more foolish they all looked.

Tower priests - the whole wisdom of Zaria. Confounded by a single Agben female.

Pinter ought to do something, say something. Rescue his master. Instead he waited on the High Priest's reply.

"You defy Yute?" Bowag shouted.

"I welcome her wisdom," the Agben smiled.

She speaks well, Pinter realized. Perhaps being out in the world, helping Terrin instead of hiding in a Tower and shouting commands, gave her an authority Zaria lacked.

Beyond her, he spied Prince Tryst. The one skin he himself had seen as key to it all - and the boy he'd ordered to be brought to him. Pinter had even commissioned a special Reeder potion, to make Prince Tryst's obedience both absolute and long-lasting. A brilliant plan to divert the course of the skins for the good of the Terrin. And it would have succeeded if Rain had done her part.

That plot must not now be exposed.

And as little as he liked Bowag, the Tower must not be exposed. Far better to protect it, to pluck the black rot from inside the walls without letting others see. There was already too much suspicion of Zaria - they might never recover from full exposure.

Behind the Prince the other skins assembled, and it gave him an idea. He rubbed the Loud Speak on his own throat.

"Gamesmen?" Pinter asked aloud, and the enhanced word echoed across the Gathering. "Yute shows her wisdom quite clearly."

The Agben turned to him, eyes narrowing above her disappearing fangs.

"The gamesmen surely came to play," Pinter smiled. "We shall let them."

The whole Gathering was in an uproar.

Marra felt the reaction in the air. Smugness from the priests, anger from Tinge, dismay from Kirth. Elation from Qwall and his men, as if they and they alone had produced the answer to a Zaria conundrum.

And Drail, damn him, was eager. Purely, boyishly

eager.

Now she perched on an old log near the trees, facing away from all the activity. Wrapping her arms about her knees, she tried not to think.

His approach cut through the madness behind her. "Marra, what do you think? Drail wants to use both the Birr Elixir and the Terrin potion. But might they not be compatible?"

She saw the toes of Tryst's boots step beside her. When had his very movement become so familiar that she recognized the sound long before his speech?

"Marra?"

She sighed. "Tis foolish to play Terrin."

"That horse has already fled the barn," he said. "We have played them several times."

"They were...amused. They indulged you. This game is for the Tower, for Zaria and their god! Can you not see the difference?"

For an answer he sat beside her, laying an arm across her shoulders. She looked up - and read in his face that he *did* see. Of course he understood - Tryst was no fool.

She ought to have swallowed her fears and kept silent.

"Drail is a great gamesman from a line of great gamesmen. He'll come to no harm."

"And you?" The words escaped before she could stop them.

His arm squeezed her shoulders. "As the Terrin will

discover, my skills are sufficient."

Are they? Marra wondered bitterly. But she had enough command of herself to keep that question between her teeth.

"The game is tomorrow, after the first meal has digested."

Drail, loosening his shoulders, grinned at Qwall, who thumped his back in approval. "You will display well."

Jason and Tryst - who'd been doing more murmuring than stretching - approached. "If we give a good game," the Prince frowned, "that says Yute smiles on us."

Drail smothered a sigh. These two had been on and on about what it all meant. Unable to just accept things as they were, to simply play.

"Agben and the Tower feud over the truths in the scrolls," Jason told him. "If you are badly thumped, that bolsters the priest's claims. But if somehow you draw a little admiration, even a tiny smile or two, they'll perceive it as their god's smile. Such a show of approval weakens Zaria's claims."

Qwall nodded. "Yute would crush you quick if she did not like you."

"If we win...." Drail began and was cut off by Qwall's bark of laughter.

"You cannot win, puny one."

"Who do we play?" Tryst asked.

Adeena strode into their midst. Pregnant with news, Drail judged by the set of her lips. News that she did not like.

"The High Priest sought the wisdom of the stones. They name the Terrin champion Murgar."

"The Bone Breaker," Jason hissed.

"Murgar's village arrived even as the stones were cast. The priests did not know."

"Of course they did not know," Tryst sighed. "They would not think to scan the Gathering or heed scouts reporting back to them."

They were worried, Drail knew. To them much hinged on this game - perhaps even the long-standing peace between the continents. Princes had responsibilities, Jason had once told him in a tavern on a different continent.

But this challenge appealed to the gamesman in him. In truth, delighted him. To test his skills....

Drail spoke aloud, and it was Raston's words, his grandsire's speech from the days in the desert, that flowed from his tongue.

"To worry about prize money has never aided victory, nor the fear of losing aim a single shot. Just play with all your strength and mind and heart. For then, whatever the outcome, tis at least an honest one."

Adeena beamed at him. For the moment, that was enough.

Kirth spoke with Tinge long into the night.

"An enhancement potion," Kirth frowned. "Does it enhance the wrong things? Should we alter it for a skin?"

Tinge's fur quivered with her answering head shake. "Enlargement, not enhancement. Somewhat delicate in its balance. It took years to perfect the formula - we dare not alter it in a single night."

Kirth sighed. Terrin potions, she had come to realize, had no division between disciplines. What exactly did the brew enlarge?

"We know the skins took it without ill effect. We know they felt more powerful, better able to play." Tinge stared into the small fire at their feet. "If we had a full cycle of moons, we might better the ingredients. With but a single night...."

Near the tree line, a sleep-sling hung peacefully. "Marra," Kirth called softly. The sleep-sling rustled; Marra appeared through its folds.

"Can you do anything with this enhancement potion?"

The child blinked owlishly. "I'll try, Mistress."

The next morning Qwall brought Marra a scarlet waterskin. She thanked him and plucked the stopper free.

As soon as the cork was drawn the odors assailed her - odors of land and Kwitt. And now she could detect the hint of Wiskett Bramble.

This brew had made the others seem larger to her - the others who had drank the potion, she realized. And it had made her seem larger to others who had not drank.

Marra threaded her way through Qwall's villagers as they laughed over their breakfast of grain balls. She nodded at Drail and Tryst without pausing to answer their calls to stop and eat.

She slipped past the gathered males to the single log near the swamp forest, where the two Agben elders nibbled their food. Marra sat at their feet.

"Wiskett Bramble," she asked. "What does it do?"

"We do not know," Kirth said.

"How would you know Wiskett Bramble?" Tinge spoke sharply.

"We have a vine planted at the school in Missea," Kirth frowned. "Rain discovered...Rain claimed to discover it on her climb down from your place. We have yet to discover a use."

Up till then Marra had only been able to read one expression on the Terrin's face - when her fangs lengthened into a grin. Yet watching the green teeth vanish beneath her drooping jowl, she knew Tinge felt angry.

"Our Rain is devious," Tinge growled. "Wiskett Bramble is an extremely potent vine. Very rare. She could only have stolen it from my private garden."

"And its use?"

"It...mirrors."

Mirrors. Marra remembered how the gamesmen had seemed to grow large before her eyes. "It *shares* the effect?" she gasped. "Causes those who have not swallowed the herb to still experience it?"

"Impossible," Kirth scoffed.

Tinge sighed. "The effect is not nearly as strong, and some herbs work better than others. But yes - it can make a reaction echo through those present. The comet juice makes one believe he is bigger, stronger. Better. A touch of Wiskett Bramble makes others believe it as well."

"If the Skin's juice had more Bramble," Kirth slowly began. "Would that make the Terrin believe it more? Tilt the balance?"

Fangs slowly lengthening, Tinge nodded. "We'd not even need to brew more juice - just add crushed Bramble to one of Qwall's stash."

Marra wasn't so sure.

She was checking the stores in her herb sash when Tryst, Drail, and Jason strode up.

"Kirth says you can enhance the Terrin brew," the Defense Master said, his shadow blocking the sun.

"We think this one can," Tinge rumbled, appearing from the other side to take a seat beside Kirth. She must have told the men.

Marra shielded her eyes to see the circle of faces. All solemn, all expectant. All waiting on her.

This would not be easy.

"You drank this before several games?" she asked. "Did it make you better?"

Drail and Tryst exchanged a look. "I felt better," Tryst said. "I felt stronger, bigger. More powerful."

"But *were* you? Stronger, I mean?"

"Of course they were!" Jason was impatient. "I could see the difference from the sidelines."

"Marra," Kirth frowned. "Never mind what I said about the third discipline. This is an exception, child."

"I think you spoke truth, Mistress."

Jason was glaring at her, but they needed to understand. "Did you play any game without the drink?" she persisted.

"Just the first," Drail spoke slowly. He was thinking - she could tell from the furrow on his brow.

"And how did you do in that game?"

His silence held as the others stared. At her, at each other.

"That was the closest we came to winning," Tryst answered slowly.

"I believe the third discipline works more on the mind than the body," Marra sighed. "It makes you feel...better. Makes you believe you're larger than you truly are. But it's really a trick. You do not actually grow at all."

"I saw...." Jason's voice tapered off.

She nodded. "We all saw King Bactor walking the Palace gardens, issuing orders. But he was not there."

"Wiskett Bramble." Kirth breathed, whirling to stare

at Tinge. "Others are trapped in the same illusion."

The Terrin slowly nodded. "You see clearly, little Marra. That is indeed what the red waterskin does."

The men gaped, shared looks. Digesting the idea, Marra thought, and had to suppress a wild desire to laugh.

It was the Defense Master who spoke first. "Are they not better off with the same potion? Equal footing?"

"Drail missed blocks he never missed at home," Marra replied. "Every play the Hand made was a hair short or a blink of the sun late. You all had as much trouble sinking a ball as the Terrin."

Tryst nodded grimly. "The only balls we sank were before we drank the potion."

"We sank one ball here...." Manten began.

"Tryst did," Jason told him. "He'd only pretended to drink."

"It distorts things!" Drail hit her shoulder painfully, but she knew it was his approval thump. "We can't accurately judge their body placement!"

"If they don't drink," Kirth stooped low beside her, "Won't it affect them all the more? Make them see the Terrin even larger, feel more fear?"

Marra smiled softly. "There is a potion that enhances the senses. It focuses mind and body...allows one to see clearly."

Drail broke into a wide grin. "The Birr Elixir."

The Birr Elixir, as Tryst remembered, needed an

hour to work properly. They had almost reached that time when Murgar and his team marched out onto the comet field.

"Mur-gar. Mur-gar." The chant arose as the champion moved, keeping pace with his hairy feet.

And the Great Goose guide him if the Terrin didn't appear the part - surely the biggest creature Tryst had yet to see. Was he truly so big - or would he shrink once Marra's brew took hold?

Drail strode out to meet him, that perpetual boyish eagerness shining from his eyes. How could the man feel so confident? Or had the gamesmen learned to hide his doubts?

Tryst felt enough doubt for both of them. Best to shake that off, for it wouldn't help him on the field.

Watching the Trumen and Terrin select their comet balls beside the darop teeth ring, Tryst felt a profound calm rise through him. If Drail could do this with such bravery....

And then Olver's face came into view. The Trumen was terrified.

So much for desert courage.

Pinter followed Bowag out into the sunshine.

The land felt bright - brighter than he'd ever seen. Or perhaps that was the result of living inside a dark tower for so long.

Too long, really. The gloom hid much, allowing doubts to fester. The very silence within isolated the priests with their own thoughts. And while Zaria walled itself off from the rest of the world, Agben lived among the people, generously sharing knowledge and skills.

Before him the mass of villagers surrounded the field, eager to watch the game. The Tower will not be able to alter this story, Pinter realized, whatever happened. Too many witnesses to tell tales of their own.

Best to hope for a resounding Terrin victory.

Murgar, the Bone Crusher, dominated the arena, the skin beside him less than a third of his mass. Far better if the champions played gently, without the brutality for which they were famed, but such would not happen. The Misseans might not survive the encounter.

Bowag turned. Pinter glimpsed a reed dart in his paw - the thin stalk of a water puff plant with the tiny puff attached to a Cack needle. The needles were dipped in poison and lethal to any creature pricked by the point.

"The Black Tower will not lose today," the High Priest said softly.

Until that moment, Pinter had felt they'd win through. That Yute would favor them and none would ever know of Bowag's plot to destroy half the creatures of the world. He'd been certain in the same way he once was certain of Zaria's wisdom. But spying the green tube of death, he felt a chill.

The High Priest, even now, could not trust to the goddess he supposedly served.

"Comet!"

Whirling, Drail hurled his ball. Even as it left his fingers, something whacked his shoulder blades. He struck the ground so hard moss shot down his nostrils.

He pushed up to glimpse Murgar loping away.

So it was one of *those* games. A game where opponents erred on the side of bodily harm rather than risk losing. He'd play a few of those - any gamesman had. But never on the Dim Continent against Terrin three times his mass.

Shoving off the turf, he discovered his lower arm was damaged...possibly broken. Drail had to balance carefully on his feet and shake off the dizziness.

Thus he saw Tryst's body arcing high into the air, slamming into the ground at a grinning Terrin's feet.

A strange hiss sound encircled them, as if angry snakes surrounded the field. Not snakes - spectators. When he saw Qwall's shaking fist, he realized they were booing the Terrin gamesmen brutality.

The crowd's reaction angered Murgar. Drail feared the result might be fatal.

Snatching a fallen comet from the ground, Murgar trotted toward the center cone. Flaming eyes locked onto Drail's as he took aim.

Oddly, the Terrin shrank before his eyes. Not due

to dizziness - but the Birr Elixir. The potion had reached full strength.

Murgar's ball shot over his head, probably intended to make him duck. Instead he caught it - fumbling as pain blasted down his injured arm. Steadying the sphere against his body, Drail turned and tossed with his good hand.

The comet arced perfectly straight into the cone.

For a blink of the sun, silence.

And then a deafening roar thundered across the field. For whatever reason, the Terrin were cheering the underdog skins. Drail smiled at the stomping creatures.

Until he saw Murgar hurtling towards him, slowing only to scoop up another ball before racing full out. Even with the Birr Elixir nullifying the enlargement potion, an all-out Terrin was a frightening thing to see. Drail bent his knees, ready to dive out of the way, but the creature was so quick he knew he'd not make it.

Thin, muscled legs drove it blindingly fast. In all his time on the Dim Continent, he'd never seen a hint these things could move like that.

Even as Drail dove to the left - fully prepared for a bone-crushing collision - Murgar staggered. A tiny flinch really, but enough to alter his coarse. The Terrin veered right, clipping Drail's legs as the monster fell.

Rolling to his feet, Drail was relieved they still supported him.

Murgar rose to hands and knees before him, the size of a small pony. Drail scooped the Terrin's lost ball - if he sank it, the game would be over.

Still on the ground, the Terrin let out a roar that echoed off the jungle. Of frustration...of pain. The massive arms trembled and gave out.

The comet dropped from his hands as Drail knelt beside the champion.

"Yute...." Murgar choked, and closed his eyes.

"Yute!" hissed the High Priest beside him. Pinter could only gape.

Bowag had actually raised the reed dart to his mouth, despite the violation of the laws of Yute, despite the risk to all the players. Instinctively Pinter had shoved it aside - a blink of the sun too late.

Already the fallen Terrin was surrounded. They'd never be able to retrieve the dart.

Marra felt smothered in the heat and the dust. The air carried a smell of baked leaves and unwashed Terrin.

She had never covered her eyes at a game, not even when the Hand of Victory faced Skullan teams. Now only clenched fists kept her from doing so when Drail hit the ground and Tryst smashed against the turf in a puff of debris.

Adeena gasped; Jason hissed through his teeth. The Defense Master grabbed her arm, either to hold her back or stop himself from racing across the field.

Relief flooded through her veins when Drail rolled upright. Surely Tryst would too, as soon as he caught his breath. Likely he was winded.

Focused on the Prince, she didn't see the Terrin's fall.

And then, as the other gamesmen stilled, as Drail knelt by the prone Terrin and Tinge hurried out to join him, she saw Jason race across the field toward Tryst.

Marra ran.

Flinging herself down beside him, knees smacking painfully on the ground, she hesitated a blink of the sun. And then reached to feel his pulse.

Tryst moaned.

"It's over, my Prince," Jason whispered.

"Did we win?"

Releasing a long held breath, Marra began to check his bones for damage.

Kirth waited as Tinge squatted beside the fallen gamesman. She could see Murgar's chest laboring to breath.

Others surrounded them. His Terrin teammates, Drail and his men, Qwall. Marra must be lost in their midst.

"Lady," Qwall rumbled softly. "What is wrong with this one?"

Tinge plucked a fluffy feather from Murgar's chest -

a feather atop a sharp barb. And despite the heat, a chill shot down Kirth's spine. She'd never seen such a thing, but could guess what it meant.

Looking across the field she saw the priests, stock still and eyes riveted on Murgar.

"Qwall," Kirth said. "Fetch the High Priest and his second."

And when the Terrin only gaped at her, Tinge glanced up and nodded.

Qwall left. And returned with the two priests. Kirth noted how he ushered them, as a sheep dog would sheep. Though the village leader never physically touched their robes, the threat was there.

The priests bristled with indignation. Beneath that seething emotion, however, Kirth sensed a profound...nervousness.

"Lady." The High Priest bowed. "You dare summon me?"

"To help your champion." Tinge's steady gaze seemed to unnerve the Terrin. Beneath his robe his body shifted from one side to the other - like an apprentice caught with a failed brew.

He shifted more rapidly as Tinge displayed the dart.

"Do you have an antidote?"

"You cannot...."

"We do," the second priest told her, and hurried away.

He returned moments later, bearing a tiny vial. Stooping, he tilted the contents into Murgar's mouth, tapping the glass bottom to be sure it emptied, and lastly rubbed a smear around the swollen dart wound.

Kirth sensed the High Priest swell with anger. His tongue, however, produced nothing more than a steamy hiss.

Which was just as well. Looking at the surrounding faces, both skin and Terrin, she doubted anyone would heed him.

Fortunately, Murgar survived.

His breathing steadied, his tremors ceased. Tinge sat back, wiping her wet forehead with her paw, before turning her gaze to the High Priest. "Why did you do this?"

His mouth spluttered, seeking a defense. "I would not...."

Qwall's paw snaked out, yanking the High Priest's hand, turning it over. Within it lay some sort of thick reed.

Kirth did not recognize it - but obviously Qwall and the others did. "A reed gun," Tinge told her. "The weapon used to deliver such darts."

The High Priest snatched his paw back.

"I am the High Priest of Zaria! I obey Yute's commands!"

Kirth felt the hesitation around her. While Tinge remained unimpressed, the male Terrin were. One must be careful questioning a priest, she realized, lest one question his god.

"FIVE SPOT!" shouted a distant voice.

The Terrin turned, allowing Kirth to see the field beyond, where the judge thrust a comet ball high in the air.

"The skins sank the five spot! They WON!"

Drail grinned as Qwall gaped.

"It would seem," Tinge rumbled softly, "Yute speaks her own mind."

By the time Tryst rose to his feet and brushed the fine gray dust from his clothes, the other village leaders had gathered. He noted the Terrin solemnly stood close enough to hear - but not too close. Wary, he supposed.

Not surprising.

The mid-day heat beat on his back, reminding him of the desert more than the jungle. The rains seemed to have cleared the heavy moisture from the air, at least for the moment.

At the thought of the desert he glanced at Marra. She'd surprised him with her hasty appearance, after avoiding him for days. Now she strode at his side, earning a frown from Jason. The Defense Master probably expected her to fall back two strides, to allow Tryst to lead. Marra didn't know that protocol.

And it was doubtful, he found himself smiling, that she would care if she did.

"FIVE SPOT!" shouted a distant voice. "The skins sank the five spot! They WON!"

Tryst smothered his laughter as the Terrin parted

before them, fangs lengthening in that peculiar grin of theirs. As the last few withdrew to reveal Kirth and Tinge confronting the two priests, he understood their silence.

The air between the women of Agben and the men of Zaria crackled with tension. The High Priest was livid - but somehow Tinge's controlled fury seemed more dangerous.

"It would seem," she rumbled softly, "Yute speaks her own mind."

"I will see you skinned...." the High Priest roared, and was silenced by Qwall's abrupt gesture.

"We revere the Tower," Qwall told him in a loud voice. A voice that carried across the Gathering crowd. "We revere Agben as well. But Agben did not attempt to murder one of us today."

The surrounding Terrin nodded. Nervous they may be, but they agreed with Qwall's words, and solidified behind him.

Marra moved to lift Drail's arm, shaking her head. Tryst realized the gamesman held it oddly. And as she frowned up at the man, he saw the same exasperated look sisters give brothers. He'd just never noticed that before.

"I have read your scrolls," Tinge said. "They were never meant to be hidden from the world, as the oldest of us well remember. Zaria's place is to tend and protect, not to subvert and hide."

"WOMAN!" the High Priest screeched, but could

find nothing more to say. Tinge allowed him to flounder before responding. Tryst had never appreciated how astute she was until then.

"The ancient text describes the world in two races, warns against the tendency for war between them. It suggests - urges - that we are stronger together than apart."

Head shaking in denial, the High Priest sputtered, "One race will die!"

"One race *could* die," Tinge growled, "If the scrolls are not heeded."

Marra, quiet little Marra who never spoke out of turn, saw it first. "Two races," she gasped. "Not Skullan and Trumen...Terrin and Skin."

The utter silence that followed proved the truth of her words.

"You see well, child," Tinge nodded. "This division between your people never existed when the scrolls were writ. It was created."

"How?" Tryst asked, somehow keeping his voice calm. "When?"

It was the second priest that answered. "Two generations back, we found a way to avert the prophecy by naming those on the desert land one thing, and those on the Great Continent another. We...encouraged the Great Continent to perceive itself as superior, and the desert dwellers to both believe and resent that idea."

Tryst felt his belly ice over. It was too wild a notion

- yet somehow it fit. "But the physical differences?"

"Early on we gave growth potions to your people. We no longer do that. It seemed that once the changes were begun, you skins managed to make more of your own. We hoped you'd war on each other, and when it appeared otherwise, some of us chose to force more conflict."

"You thought to busy us fighting each other?" Jason stared from one to the other. "But you're stronger than us, in many ways. Were you so frightened?"

It was Tinge who answered him. "Terrin are physically stronger - but deeply suited to a simple life. Calm and predictable. Our males are cautious of each other; more so of outsiders. We've never united under any leader, despite Zaria's attempts."

"Even in a game of comet," Marra's eyes lit up. "The skins managed to win the day."

A roar of laughter burst from Qwall's lungs. "You did indeed," he rumbled when he could speak.

9.

AS KIRTH HELD her skirts high to keep from treading on the hem, she felt the chill air swirl around her ankles. Reminding her of the last time she followed a priest down these steps, to find herself in a cell with the door swinging shut. If she were a fanciful woman, she might insist upon sitting in the warm sun while the matter was brought to her.

By the Great Goose, she was not a fanciful woman.

Still, when the priest lead her to another cell, holding the torch aloft to reveal the unyielding metal grid, a pang of fear shot through her veins.

And then she saw Rain.

The woman's face pressed against the metal, eyes wild, the long hair she'd been so proud of now matted and dirty. Despite everything - lies, betrayal, even murder - Kirth felt pity.

"Have you come to gloat, old woman?" Rain spat. So she hadn't quite lost all her backbone.

"I've come seeking answers," Kirth said. The priest set the torch in a nearby bracket and withdrew into the dark.

"Why should I tell you anything?"

Kirth sighed. "Rain, we still have to decide what to do with you. King Bactor might well execute you for treason."

She said nothing, but Kirth felt her stiffen. So that thought hadn't occurred - in fact she still expected to be released. Arrogance was ever her downfall.

"I can make other choices. But they must be made soon."

Rain's mouth squeezed into a tight line. Whether holding back angry words or a hasty tale Kirth could only guess.

So she turned as if to leave.

"What would you know?" the younger woman whispered.

Her story emerged, prodded on by gentle questions. Exactly how much was fact and how much was fiction Kirth could guess. Still, she told a reasonable tale.

It seemed to begin on the woman's first lone journey to the Dim Continent. Visiting the false Zaria Tower with Tinge, she pried into the scrolls while the Terrin was outside gathering herbs. These scrolls were blank, which lead to troubling questions.

And Pinter, hiding to keep an eye on her, caught her spying.

From there he tempted her with information, power. Her yearly pilgrimage became a furthering indoctrination. Pinter's association with her advanced him to the Tower, and when he brought her to Bowag, the High Priest offered to spare Agben if she helped him.

Or so she said.

Kirth believed Rain's true motivation was power. Feeling powerless as a young girl, she had ever sought it since.

"How involved was Britta?" she asked, when the woman had fallen silent. That silence held for three blinks of the sun.

And then, "I sent her three missives," Rain muttered. "She answered the first by ordering me to lay the whole story before you. To the second, when I explained it was the only way to preserve Agben, she never answered."

"And the third?"

Rain sniffed. "In the third I informed her that the Prince was caught and deep in sleep...and would be delivered to her in a matter of moons."

"Why send him to the desert?"

"Bowag demanded him at the Black Tower; Britta said not to trust Zaria at all. I thought sending the sleeping man to her would answer well - she'd have no choice but to take him."

"And Fenna?"

Rain frowned.

"We found the King," Kirth told her softly, keeping her own anger in check. Had Rain thought she still had a bargaining chip?

"Fenna always jumped where Britta pointed. I hinted at the old woman's involvement and she never questioned it." The younger woman lowered her head, no doubt watching Kirth beneath her lashes. "So what will you do with me?"

"That's not up to me. You committed treason against the Skullan Empire." Kirth turned to leave.

"Agben must make this decision. The King and his little son need know nothing about it."

Rain, Kirth decided, had no real concept of what she'd done. "I'm afraid Prince Tryst is both here and knows all. He does not view your actions as so...innocuous."

The priest removed the torch from its holder. Kirth glimpsed Rain's face, eyes wide, mouth open, before the dungeon shadows claimed her.

If Tryst held any lingering concerns about Terrin aggression, the speed at which the Gathering dispersed put them to rest.

By the second day only a handful of villages remained, packing gear and swapping stories. The night before had seen a generous flow of the intoxicating mawk, rendering loud jibes and banter, as if the entire Terrin population had heaved a collective sigh of relief. He'd seen Marra across the campfire, but failed to secure her for a private conversation.

He thought they'd talk instead during the long voyage home. The Dim Continent, however, would not allow that. "You passed through the Creesby gate - you must do so again. It causes...confusion otherwise." He'd been told this by both Adeena and Qwall. It only bothered him when he learned Marra must return a different route.

Precisely what the route was, he did not know. But it started in the opposite direction from the Gathering field.

This morning, as the sun breeched the tree line, Qwall's men rolled sleep-slings and stuffed provisions into travel sacks. Everywhere he looked, the remaining Terrin prepared to leave.

Pinter and Bowag returned, with Pinter leading the way. Bowag, now clad in white, moved solemnly at his heel, even keeping his head down when Pinter spoke.

"We wish you well on your journey, Prince Tryst of the Skins. May Yute always smile upon your path."

"And yours," Tryst inclined his head. He glanced at former High Priest, who never met his eyes.

"Before being accepted to priest," Pinter said, "A male proves himself worthy by humbly - and nimbly - doing as commanded by those he would join. Teaching servitude so to serve Yute."

Tryst stared at the former High Priest.

"Bowag will remain at this level to serve the Tower. To remind us that service must swallow ego. And what happens when ego swallows service."

Tinge, Kirth, and Marra joined them. "And what of Rain?" Kirth asked.

"Rain will be surrendered to Tinge," the priest said.

Tinge smiled. "Our Rain will benefit sharing this lesson of service."

Tryst didn't welcome this news. Rain had betrayed his people and his family; fetch and carrying seemed far too small a punishment. "Where is Rain?" he asked.

Something in his tone must have told of his thoughts.

"She remains in her cell," Tinge replied. "To be freed, she must take the Promise Potion."

"Promise...?"

"One swears the promise, drinks the entire bottle swiftly, and swears it again," Tinge explained. "If that promise is ever broken, the potion turns to poison."

He hoped to ask Marra about it later, but seeing her surprise, realized it was just as new to her.

"How long does the effect last?" Kirth frowned.

Tinge's fangs lengthened. "We have only tested it for a century. There was no diminishing of effect in that span."

The Tower Terrin left, and shortly thereafter, so did the rest. Tryst only had time to take Marra's hand and smile reassuringly before Qwall and Jason pulled him one way as Kirth drew her the other.

The soft smile she gave him in parting would have to sustain Tryst for a handful of moons.

The trek back to Creesby was bittersweet.

Drail and Adeena appeared close by the time they reached the gate. With his arm in a sling, she found many opportunities to help him. Yet when the time came to part, neither seemed to hold regret.

Of course, Tryst himself was preoccupied. The gatekeeper demanded two counts, with a third one performed by his companion. When Adeena asked for an explanation, he told her a lone skin had appeared days earlier, claiming to have been shipwrecked on the Dim Continent.

They'd locked the man away until all groups had returned and been properly counted. The man, it turned out, was Kratchett.

The gatekeepers turned him over to Jason.

Kratchett offered more information, about Lump and a cohort on the Flats of Beard - a Trumen named Snark.

"In Marra's shop in San Cris," Drail frowned. "Nasty guy - I punched him hard."

"Not hard enough," Kratchett told them. "He killed his own sister...I think she was Agben. Name of Britta."

For Marra the journey home was half the time of the voyage to the Dim Continent. Something about the direction of currents and wind.

Another moon passed before Drail and Tryst arrived in Missea. Drail sent a missive to the school, telling her of a game that afternoon. Preparing the Birr Elixir, she went.

Their first full day back, yet Drail and the Hand of Victory not only played, but won. The first of several surprises.

"Now we travel the Great Continent," Drail grinned. "We need only Marra, and Fallon's replacement."

The gamesman was smiling down at her, warmth and laughter in his eyes. Perhaps it was that, or perhaps watching him win against the Trumen just as he'd won against the Terrin that gave her the courage.

For she knew her own heart, and found the courage to own it.

"Drail, forgive me," Marra told him. "I need to continue my studies. May I brew you some elixir to take with you instead?"

His eyes glinted gold. Surprised, she thought, but not unhappy. "Forgive *me*, little Marra," he touched her shoulder. "I forget you have your own life to live. We'll come see you as soon as we return - and swap tales of our adventures for yours."

Leah, standing arm in arm with Fallon, giggled. "I'd love to play Brista and come traveling with you," she said. "Why did you not tell me?"

Fallon stared at her. "I did not think you would wish to leave the Agben School."

"Now that Kirth is home, I can please myself for a

time."

Returning to the school with Leah later, Marra worried what Kirth herself would say to this scheme. She was startled to find the elder only smiled. "Thank goodness we have a new teacher starting next week."

She presented Marra a tiny box carved of Sandalwood. When Marra lifted the lid, a silver dove gleamed within.

Leah hugged her. "You're no longer a student," she whispered. "You're Agben!"

Marra stole a look at Kirth - surely there must be a mistake. But the elder actually smiled.

"You have earned this," she said. "Marra, you are indeed a full-grown Woman of Agben."

After the evening meal, as twilight sought to drive the sun from the sky, Marra stood on the balcony of her palace chamber. She'd come to retrieve a favorite mortar and pestle, and found herself lingering to enjoy the garden. With her new teaching duties, visiting the lovely grounds might be rare.

And she'd miss them, she realized. The palace had always felt too above her station - but perhaps that was a flaw in her mind. It was after all nature, like Agben's gardens. Just more organized and less varied.

"Marra." Karna, the young Skullan girl, appeared below her. "How nice to see you! Come walk with me?"

And despite the inelegance of the move, Marra

climbed the railing to hop down beside her.

"I am in love," Karna said.

A pang hit Marra's heart. "With Tryst?"

The girl glanced at her before shaking her head. "No. He's too short and too young. I prefer someone with authority. *Him*."

Marra looked up to see Jason and Tryst approaching. "You mean...?"

"Yes," Karna nodded, and skipped forward to wrap her arm around the Defense Master's. With a giggle, she tugged the man down a different path.

Startled, Marra met Tryst's eyes. His reflected the same surprise.

"I think Jason likes her," Tryst said.

"It's mutual," Marra told him, and found herself laughing. "He has more authority, and you are too short."

As soon as the words were out her cheeks flamed. But Tryst didn't seem to take offense.

"Jason tells me there is a reason I am so short. One my Grandsire intended to keep from me."

Marra turned to him, frowning. His hand cupped her cheek as if to keep her there.

"My mother, it seems, was Trumen."

She gasped.

"My father and I share similar tastes."

Gently, very gently, he kissed her again. As he'd done in the goss jungle on the Dim Continent.

"There is a way to end the tension between our two

people," he murmured. "Their prince could marry a Trumen apprentice."

Marra stared up at him, her mind full of reasons to refuse, to push away. But her heart ignored them all.

"I am a Woman of Agben," was all she said.

"So much the better."

They were married in a royal ceremony that beggared all celebrations. Marra did not really like it, but Tryst explained that some things must be when one is a prince.

Drail and the Hand of Victory delayed their journey until after the wedding. "I am glad for you, little desert sister," Drail told her before kissing her cheek. They hugged for a long time.

Marra kept her room at the Agben School, where she taught as well as continued her studies. She used the space to store Agben items. Tryst frowned at that idea, but Marra explained that some things must be when one is a Woman of Agben.

Tryst's mother had indeed been Trumen, and had apparently kept a Trumen lady in waiting as her personal dressmaker. Marra wondered about her own mother, a dressmaker with skills far beyond the desert town where she grew up. But she could never find the slightest evidence.

Not that it mattered.

For they all lived, despite the tiny challenges life presents to each of us, very happily indeed. King Bactor welcomed her with open arms, and if King

Ganny was not so inclined at first, he forgave all when the new prince was born. For the boy, he declared to the world, would grow to the Skullan stature with the Trumen grit. Providing the Empire a promising future indeed.

And no one dared argue with that.

End of Book 3 & End of Story

THE BIRR ELIXIR

Book 1 of The Legend of the Gamesmen

Marra never heard of Birr Elixir. But when Drail sees the potion in her dead mistress's book, she agrees to make it. Even lacking the right ingredient.

And after drinking it, Drail and his men defeat a Skullan team - something no one has ever done before. Marra is offered a place as his traveling potions mistress. Full of doubts of her own ability, she takes the chance to escape her slave-like existence.

Then her potions woke a man who was not supposed to wake.

Now every day draws more attention from the True Masters. And their motives – and morals – are not for the faint of heart.

If they discover the truth ...

THE AGBEN SCHOOL

Book 2 of The Legend of the Gamesmen

It should have been a happy ending.

A Prince restored, victory in the black arena. Instead the band of friends shatters against an evil conspiracy.

Refusing to endanger one man or burden another, Marra flees to the Agben School. Agben, whose ancient walls have held for a thousand years, protecting those within as they sought to harness the power of nature.

But this evil is relentless, and the school may not be the safe ground she thought. In fact it may not be anything she thought. Cut off from the only friends she knew, Marra discovers more than her life hangs in the balance.

For the future of her race – of both races – depends not on a prince trying to save his people, nor the heroic men who'd brought them this far.
Everything depends on *her*.

ABOUT THE AUTHOR

Jo Sparkes, a well-known Century City Producer once said, *"...writes some of the best dialogue I've read."*

Jo graduated from Washington College, a small liberal arts college famous for its creative writing program, and went on to study with Robert Powell: a student of renowned teachers Lew Hunter and Richard Walter, head of UCLA's Screenwriting Program.

She's won a Kay Snow for her comedy script, 'Frank Retrieval', a Silver IPPY for 'The Birr Elixir', and BRAG Medallions for multiple books. A member of the Pro Football Writers Association, she was (unofficially) the first to interview Emmitt Smith when he came to the Arizona Cardinals.

Jo served as an adjunct teacher at the Film School at Scottsdale Community College, and even made a video of her most beloved lecture. Her book for writers and artists, "Feedback How to Give It How to Get It" has garnered strong praise.

When not diligently perfecting her craft, Jo can be found exploring her new home of Portland, Oregon, with her husband Ian, and their dog Oscar.

www.ingramcontent.com/pod-product-compliance
Lightning Source LLC
Chambersburg PA
CBHW030629110726
47901CB00002B/380